BODY IN THE PARK

A RITA PATEL MYSTERY

By Catherine Cooper

ISBN 978-1-910779-68-2

This story is a work of fiction and the characters and events in them exist only in these pages and in the author's imagination.

Typeset and published by
Oxford eBooks Ltd.
www.oxford-ebooks.com

Oxford eBooks

Chapter

1

"I am now a condemned traitor . . . I am to die when I have hardly begun to live."

Attributed to Lady Jane Grey

9ᵗʰ August 2012

Nothing is happening. The air is still. The evening has stalled between daylight and sunset. Rita Patel stares out at the empty street from the bedroom of her house at 10 Elm Drive, Strictly speaking, the house belongs to her parents, Jahi and Padma, who, as Rita reminds her regularly, used money lent to them by Padma's parents to pay for it. Aged 16, Rita is their middle child; her brothers are 3 years older than her (Mohal) and 2 years younger (Nayan). The remaining streaks of sun have moved to behind the detached house, which is built, as if by a child's bricks, with a triangular top on a square base, the triangle decorated in black and white stripes, mock Tudor style, although the house was built in the reign of the second Queen Elizabeth. Rita's room, at the front, is cast in shadow but it is not yet dark enough for her to close the pink blinds which adorn her window, or for the street lamp outside her room to have come on. Rita's iPod is shuffling amongst Lady Ga Ga, Pink, Justin Bieber, Olly Murs and various former X-factor winners. She is Skyping with her school friend, Priya. This is why she fails to hear the rising crescendo of her mother's voice in the kitchen below.

"So I'm, like, 'whatever', and he's, like, 'really? think about it' and I think 'get a life, like I'm going to start imagining what it was like to be in the past, isn't it enough to learn about it…'" says Rita.

"But you don't say that?" Priya replies.

"'Course not, this is Mr Thatcher innit? What's he gonna say to Mum & Dad when… Hey, what's that on your nails?"

"Borrowed Meera's polish didn't I?"

"Great colour. Wish I had an older sister and not two brothers….We should try to get to a nail bar."

"Yeah, like in Eastenders. I'd love a French manicure. I wouldn't get away with it though." Priya says.

"Rita, come and help with the table, Bandhu and Jaina will be here soon!" After a couple of tries, Padma sighs, wipes flour from her hands, and sets off up the spiral stair case in the centre of the house.

Shouting "Rita!" immediately outside the bedroom door achieves the effect Padma desires.

"Got to go, Mum's calling, think if we could find a way to get to a nail bar, yeah?"

"Laters!" Priya signs off too.

Rita opens her bedroom door, her face formed into an innocent, inquiring, expression, as she suspects that Padma has called her before.

"Yes, Mum?"

"What are you doing in here?" Padma tries to peer round the bedroom door through her designer frames – the brown rectangular shape is an improvement on the round rimless ones she used to sport, Rita thinks. Her mother has her view blocked by Rita, although she has nothing to hide. "I need you to help me with the table." Padma adds.

"Just looking at my holiday history reading." Rita invents; as she was talking to Priya about the History teacher, Mr Thatcher, it's almost true.

"The Opening Ceremony will be on later, come and get the table ready so we can see it together." Padma turns to go back to the kitchen.

Of course, Rita recalls, the 'family meal' her mother has planned so they can all watch the opening ceremony for the

London Olympics, with her aunt, uncle and cousins, on the new flat screen TV in the family kitchen which has been her mother's pet project for the last 18 months. ("Where should the island go, Jahi? Have you seen the new tile shop near Fosse Park? I've found a great fridge/freezer in the sale and they'll keep it for me until the work is done…".) This had been the background hum to Rita's recent domestic life and to her GCSE revision. When she left the house to walk round the corner to school for an exam, workers were in the kitchen area and would wish her luck; and when she returned they would ask how it went? her parents meanwhile were at the dental practice all day - as Rita puts it, "gaping into strangers' mouths" - and left Mohal in charge - the least responsible member of the family, thinks Rita.

Rita follows her mother across the landing ("Why do I have to have the smallest room? Why not one of the boys?" this was her constant grievance. "But you have an en-suite!" this is always Nayan's riposte). Mother and daughter pass, on their left, Rita's parents' room, the family bathroom and Nayan's room, then they turn to go downstairs, with Mohal's room (also en-suite) on the other side of the stairs, above the garage. ("You should have the smallest room, girls get married before boys." Mohal argues, "Just got to wait for the parents to find some poor chap to take you on!" he would add, instinctively ducking in anticipation of an object flying from Rita's hand towards his head.)

As she expects, her brothers are in the family kitchen already, using the large flat screen TV to play 'Grand Theft Auto' ("Is that suitable for Nayan?" their mother had feebly inquired) on Mohal's Xbox. They make a funny pair to look at, Rita thinks. At 19 Mohal has, to adopt her uncle's expression, outgrown his strength; he is tall and slight, like an etiolated plant. By contrast, Nayan is 14 and stubby-looking, still waiting for his major growth spurt. "Switch that off now." barks her mother, at the same time tightening the ponytail in which she keeps her thick brown wavy hair. Rita hears the panic in her tone that denotes the preparation of a 'relaxing family meal'.

"Bandhu and Jaina will be here soon!" Padma exclaims.

These were her mother's sister and her husband and no doubt they would be bringing her precocious twin cousins with them. Often, Rita found herself staring at the 12 year olds' perfect complexions, the tidy plaits in their hair and their crisp clothes and thinking how great it would be for them to be 16 like her and realise there is more to life than extra maths and hockey at the weekends. (While her cousins, Shreya and Shona, had inherited her aunt's oval face and slender, graceful looking limbs, Rita was aware she was the beneficiary of Padma's rounder features and shorter arms and legs. Furthermore, Rita's hair was very undisciplined, despite frequent use of her hair straighteners. "Use them anymore and you'll go bald!" was Mohal's familiar lack of reassurance.)

The kitchen - Padma's pride and joy - white throughout with a grey tiled floor (heated underneath) and granite work surfaces - has been extended into the garden with glass doors that slide back to give access to the patio. There, that morning, Jahi had arranged the wicker furniture in the hope that the evening would be balmy enough to enable their visitors to sit outside and admire the neat garden with raised beds that he had planted after watching endless hours (so it seemed to Rita) of Alan Titchmarsh, Monty Donn and the Chelsea flower show. Alas, there had been a lot of rain in the last two weeks and, although tonight looked like being drier, it was not a warm enough night for sitting out. And this was August!

The table in the kitchen has room for ten, three down each side and two at each end and Rita lays the places, absorbing the odours of her mother's bhajis, naan, rice and vegetable jalfrezi. Nayan is in the garden, practising off spin

("That boy is obsessed with sport" her aunt said when she visited last - she really did not understand boys). Rita is unsure where Mohal has disappeared to; having failed to get into uni last year ("You did not work hard enough for the grades." Jahi told him, exasperated) he had adopted a rather lackadaisical approach to life and apart from his Saturday job as an assistant at the Central library did not seem to do much other than play Xbox with those of his friends who had similarly fallen short of expectations ("I don't know where the food goes." Padma would say). He now had a place at Hertfordshire University for September and Padma and Jahi had been there to look at his accommodation, which they pronounced satisfactory.

"How can we all watch the ceremony?" Rita asks, not unreasonably, as not all the places at the table face the screen.

"Bandhu and Jaina are coming at seven thirty and the ceremony does not start until nine." comes the swift response. "Danny Boyle insisted on it so the fireworks will look good." Rita thinks her mother makes it sound like she is on the organising committee for the Games.

* * *

"Pass your plate, Rita." The meal is over and her mother's voice breaks Rita's fantasy in which her perfect cousins, sitting opposite her at the white table, were belly dancing on stage with Britney Spears at the O2. "I want to get the dishwasher stacked before the athletes come into the stadium." Her mother makes the filling of the dishwasher sound like an Olympic event itself.

"Oh, what dishwasher did you get?" Jaina, Padma's dutiful younger sister, picks up her cue to admire another part of Padma's great project, her neatly cut bob swinging as she turns her head to look, its auburn shades, accentuated by chemical help, shining in the beams from her sister's downlighters.

Jaina and Bandhu live in a less leafy part of Leicester, near the General Hospital, in a two bedroom house with a kitchen so small that Padma's American style fridge/freezer would practically fill it. It is her twins, Shona and Shreya, who are Jaina's pride and joy; they go to the local private school where Jaina works as the Head's PA. Jaina is already thinking how difficult it may be for her and Bandhu to find suitable husbands for both girls. She wonders what Padma's plan is for Rita, as her sister never broaches the subject, the boys and their future being her main concern, apparently.

"Put the TV on ready, Jahi," Padma is directing in her kitchen. Everyone settles into chairs or on the L-shaped sofa except the twins who sit giggling together on cushions on the floor ("Is it really heated aunty?") Rita is relieved to see that Bandhu, who is a heavily-built man compared to her father's fine features and a light frame, is settled into the robust arm chair in the corner - removing her fears for her mother's new furniture. "And now for the news where you are." the newsreader intones before the Midlands logo appears: a lorry has crashed on the M6 causing tailbacks; plans are progressing for the development of a new library in Birmingham ("Lucky them!" Shona and Shreya say); local sports personalities are tipped to do well in the Games ("Doubt it" says Nayan) and "Police say that the remains of a body have been discovered in Bradgate Country Park. The skeleton, found near the Newtown Linford entrance to the Park by the archaeological team who are digging in the area, is thought to be relatively recent and not of ancient origin."

"Thank goodness!" says Mohal surprisingly, then explains, "All that fuss going on about Richard the Third, we don't want them to find another buried royal!"

"Ssh" says Nayan "This sounds interesting. Maybe someone got topped?"

"I knew you should not play that game with Mohal," says Padma.

"Maybe it's some old person who wandered into the park and got lost." This from Bandhu, who had worked in a care home in the past before rising to his current post as a health administrator.

"Police say they have yet to establish how long the body has been there." The newsreader changes tone from serious to light, 'The archaeologists' project is of course part of our regular Monday feature and we will bring you coverage of their discoveries next week. And now, the weather; are we in for a clear night for the Opening Ceremony, Caroline?"

* * *

A week later and Nayan shouts from his room, "Will we get more medals today? Can't wait to see Mo Farah tonight!"

"Is that Nayan I can hear?" Priya and Rita are in their respective bedrooms, talking on their mobile phones. Rita closes her bedroom door to shut out the sound of her brother.

"What a loud voice he has!" says Priya.

"Tell me about it! I could do without his commentary on the Olympics, it's only running and swimming and stuff. Boring!" replies Rita.

"Yeh, but it is in London, innit... Pity we didn't get tickets in the ballot".

"I s'pose. Can you come round tonight?"

"No way" this, emphatically from Priya. "Mum's got me on a tight rein while they make the final plans for Meera's wedding. And they certainly don't want me in the same house as Mohal."

"Why not? He is a librarian. That's very respectable!" Rita is teasing her friend.

"Only on a Saturday!" said Priya.

"Wish we could get away," this from Rita who was always eager to do new things,

"Yeh. Other girls get to go on holiday after GCSEs. Trust

us to have parents who won't let us out of their sight!" Priya joins in her friend's frustration while reaching into her bag for her comb to address her hair, which she wears in long, brown bunches either side of her head. Frequently combing her hair is a habit she acquired in childhood.

"There must be something interesting we can do. It's so boring being stuck at home just waiting for exam results." Rita again. Then, "Hang on, I can hear the doorbell."

"That's odd, it's 5 o'clock." says Priya.

"Call you back." Rita hangs up and runs to the top of the open spiral stair case which is another of Padma's successful projects. She hangs over the post at the top from where she can see the back of Mohal's head as he opens the inner and outer doors of the double glazed entrance to the house.

Two people are standing on the paved drive; one is a fair-haired woman in trousers with a waterproof jacket over her white shirt, the other is a man in uniform. Meter readers? Bus drivers? (Why did she think of that?) No, she realises who they are, just as they announce themselves.

"Mr Patel? We are police officers." (Rita thinks, Nayan must have been up to something.)

"I see, your parents are not in." Mohal has explained he is not responsible for the house but spoke so softly that Rita did not hear a thing he said. The woman continues "Can you ask them to contact me when they come in please. It's nothing to do with you or your family, we just want some background to the house."

"The house?" Rita is starting to see why Mohal fits in well at the library, where you need to be quiet; conversation with strangers is clearly not one of his best skills.

"Yes. You may have heard that a body was found in Bradgate Park last week? It appears likely that it belongs to a young lady who lived here a long time ago."

"Oh" is all that Mohal can manage. Rita rushes round the curves of the staircase to see if she can find out more.

"Who was she?" she asks, adding "Hi, I'm Rita, I live here too."

The two police officers exchange glances, shrugging their shoulders." Well, you'll find out soon through the papers so I'll tell you now. Her name was Claire Watson, she was 16 when she was last seen; that was in 1972. We have reason to believe the body is hers. I'll leave you my contact details, so your parents can get in touch."

The woman hands a card to Rita who has pushed herself in front of Mohal. "Good bye now."

"Goodbye" Mohal manages.

"Weird" is his next one word sentence when he has closed the doors.

"Yes" says Rita, holding the card against her face thoughtfully. "Claire Watson, 40 years ago, living in this house."

"Don't know what the parents can say, we don't know anything about her." Mohal shakes his head, preparing to return to the fantasy world of crime on his Xbox.

"No." says Rita "But you have to admit it's interesting. I wonder what I can find out. Who was she? What happened to her?"

Chapter

2

"Out of obedience to you and my mother I have grievously sinned. Now I willingly relinquish the crown. May I not go home?"

Lady Jane Grey

12th February 1972

When the blow came, it took Claire by surprise. She'd gone in expectation of being welcomed, of kind hands extended to her, and had walked to the rendezvous with happy anticipation. Was it the force of the hand that caused her to stagger backwards, the shock of the contact with her face, her platform boots slipping in the damp mulch beneath her feet or her maxi coat flapping round her legs impeding movement? Whatever the catalyst, losing her fight with her balance, and catching her heel on a tree root as she floundered, she fell. As she did so, she tried to think how this could have happened, but she did not have long to puzzle it out. Her unprotected head hit a hard rock hidden under the bracken and her brain began to shut down.

* * *

Earlier that day, as she dressed to go out, Claire admired the smooth look and feel of her hips under the C&A skirt as she looked at herself in her mother's dressing table mirror. With the skirt, she wore the red roll neck jumper she had bought at Leicester market, against which, swaying between her breasts as she moved, she wore a round, bronze-coloured, medallion with a picture of a horse on it, a present from her aunt.

She went back to her own room to put on the black patent boots she had got from Dolcis with money saved from her Saturday job there, delighting in the process of lacing them up and feeling like one of those saloon girls in Alias Smith and Jones, her favourite TV programme at the moment. Her brown maxi coat and long orange scarf, which she had knitted herself on large knitting needles, completed her outfit. She wound it several times round her neck, taking care not to disturb the French pony tail in her fair hair, which she had decorated with elasticated black plastic bobbles. She picked up the handbag she'd bought in a jumble sale, and in which she had put her pink comb and beaded purse. She was ready to leave. She looked round quickly at her room – taking in the clothes on hangers, no room for a wardrobe, the display shelf in the shape of a noughts and crosses grid which held the tiny china ornaments she had gathered over her 16 years, mostly from Christmas crackers and Girl Guide jumble sales. Her Jackie comics, second hand from Christine Campbell who lived across the road and all well-thumbed, were piled precipitately against the far wall. The curtains were dark velvet – hard to say in what colour – they had not been made for her room and did not quite close, so that however hard she tried there was always a shaft of light from the street lamp outside her room piercing through. She left the curtains open, although it was still dark outside, not helped by the fog which was swirling around.

Claire took a last look at the letter Alex had posted to her, then placed it in her jewellery box. Everything must look as if she'd just gone off to her Saturday job as usual. She left no note for her mother (Melanie) who was at work or for her father (Philip) and her younger brothers, who were at the swimming baths. As she closed the back door (her father did not like them using the front door, she never knew why) the phrase 'Il fait du brouillard' came to her mind. French would be useful if they went to Paris! She thought.

She walked carefully for a few steps, unsure if there would be icy patches on the pavement and testing how far she could see in the fog. The grey density of the air did not trouble her, she had walked to the bus stop so often she could probably do it blindfold! It was eerie to hear footsteps coming towards her before she could see who it was, however. Claire could only really see them as they passed her. This time it was Mr Gregson, from number 8, the house next door to hers in Elm Drive, with a newspaper under his arm. He seemed to smile when he saw it was her, but it was hard to tell under his bushy moustache. As she turned in to Beech Grove she thought she could make out Mrs Campbell from number 5, opposite her house, out walking her poodle. It was a very excitable dog and when Claire came back from school she often heard it barking against the gate in the Campbell's front garden. "Oh, hello Claire" said Mrs Campbell, her Scottish accent evident even in so short a greeting, "Terrible weather!" then the fog made her disappear again, like a conjuring trick. Would the bus be running? Claire suddenly thought. Usually they did, but what if, today of all days, it did not come?

She need not have worried. As she rounded the next corner she could see the shape of the bus at the terminus, brooding in the gloom like a ghostly galleon in a pirate story. She stepped onto it lightly, grateful for its comforting interior lights and to be able to see further than a few yards again. She went upstairs in case the bus got busy, though it did not seem very likely at this early hour and with the weather so bad. The bus conductor came up immediately after her. "Single to town." She said and offered the exact money, which she had taken from her purse as soon as she sat down.

"You shopping? Meeting someone?" he asked. She looked at him properly for the first time – he was youngish, about the same age as Alex, she thought. (Alex seemed very grown up to Claire. They'd met at the shoe shop, where he worked 6 days a week, travelling to and from the shop on his motor bike.) Maybe the conductor was 19 or so? And not English looking. He looked like he was from Pakistan or India? There were lots of people like him living in the centre of town, and on the roads leading out of it now; she had seen the sari shops and Asian food markets spreading their way down Evington Road when she had visited her friend Lynn on the bus. He was one of the immigrants her father ranted about unpleasantly, but she ignored what Philip said - live and let live that was her motto. He seemed in no hurry to issue her a ticket. He was leaning jauntily against the silver pole that ran between the floor and roof of the bus, near the stairs, his ticket machine hanging over his left hip.

"Where you going today?" he tried again.

"Just town." She looked him in the eye when she said this, not sure why he was asking; she had given him the right money. She wished the bus would hurry up and go, so someone else could get on and she would not be alone with this man.

"Work." she lied (well usually she would be going to the shoe shop on a Saturday so why not stick to that?).

"Oh." Then "When you finish?"

So that's how it was, she thought, he wants me to meet him.

Before she could answer, the bus engine growled into life and the bus lurched forward, causing the conductor to end his nonchalant leaning and clutch at the pole to keep his balance.

"My boyfriend meets me when I finish." She hoped this would put him off.

"Oh, you're young to have a boyfriend!" Was he teasing her? She did not know what to say.

The bus was climbing the hill unsteadily, overhanging trees cracking branches against the front windows as it passed by, the sound was made more eerie by the poor visibility. Thank goodness, the bus stopped to let two men get on, who both came upstairs as they wanted to smoke. The conductor finally clipped out the tiny square of coloured paper which was her ticket and absent-mindedly handed it to her while simultaneously checking the mirror at the top of the stairs and ringing the bell for the bus to continue its journey.

When she reached the town centre, Claire caught the next bus from St Margaret's bus station, seeing no one she knew. The conductor was an incurious woman this time. The fog continued thick and swirling, getting denser in the countryside than in the town so that it was hard to see when they were reaching Newtown Linford. She was not troubled by the fog. It was not unusual for it to last all day at this time of year. It was just a question of not missing him at their meeting place!

Chapter

3

*"The faith of the church must be tried by God's word,
and not God's word by the church; neither yet my faith."*
Lady Jane Grey

27th August 2012

"Slow down, Mohal!", Rita is giving instructions from the back of Mohal's Peugeot, with Priya beside her. It is August Bank Holiday Monday so the Newtown Linford entrance to Bradgate Park, which they are approaching, is as busy as the town centre car parks on a Saturday. Most of the people who are out walking to and from the parkland are casually dressed and, as the weather is, unusually, pleasant, there are bare arms and legs on display, mostly pink but some brown, protruding from T shirts and shorts or skirts; the T shirts are of various colours but the majority have writing on, some relating to products like beer or soap, some giving out messages which may be intended to be inspirational or ironical, it was hard to tell, including variations on the over-used 'Keep Calm' slogan from the second world war. Rita catches sight of one which makes her laugh. The rather puny chest of a stubble-chinned ginger-haired boy of about her age bares the legend "I'm up and I'm dressed, what more do you want?" which seems appropriate for 2.30 in the afternoon and a recognisable sentiment from her experience of her brothers.

As she spots the entrance to the car park Rita says "Go in there!"

"Oh Rita," Mohal protests "You can see how busy it is."

"But we're not parking" she replies.

"Yeh, can't leave the car in these outfits! My shoes wouldn't last two minutes on the paths there." this from Priya.

Both girls are brightly and magnificently adorned in saris, Priya's a silvery mauve colour, Rita's a bright turquoise. The crystals and sequins sewn into them glitter in the afternoon light as Mohal (also well-turned out) steers into the car park and the sun streams across the back of the car. As the car turns, the movement causes the bracelets covering the arms of both girls to ripple with a satisfying chiming sound. If she ducks her head, Rita can see herself in the rear view mirror, her large gold hooped earrings shining against her face bright with make-up and her hair behaving for once, she is pleased to note.

People are spilling out of their cars, those planning picnics arming themselves with cool boxes and rugs. But Rita is not really noticing them. She is looking intently out of the window of the Peugeot, taking in, as they approach it, the wooden fence and gateway through which you walk (if you had on sensible shoes and weren't dressed for a wedding) to get into Bradgate Park. Scrabbling in her Cath Kidston bag ("Sure you've brought enough?" Mohal being sarcastic again). She takes out her phone and clicks a few pictures to download later. The path broadens as it climbs gradually into the distance. Somewhere, Rita knows, are the ruins of an old house; in the distance is a folly on a high hill which everyone calls 'Old John', she doesn't know why. ("Lady Jane Grey, the 9 day Queen!" Nayan had said excitedly when he heard they were going to sneak out to Bradgate Park. "Don't tell anyone and I won't mention you've got your Nintendo DS with you." was the deal Rita had struck with him. "We did that in junior school; we went on a trip there." He helpfully added.)

The ground surrounding the path is a carpet of bracken, fringed by trees. Fronds in a surprising variety of shades of green are intertwined, some of them would probably turn to a pale orange or yellow in the autumn and maybe even brown by mid-winter, which was when Claire had disappeared; Rita knew this from what the police had said. The bracken looks soft and wispy, almost eerie, as though it holds secrets. But was she imagining that, knowing that the poor girl's body had lain there, undisturbed, for so many years? There was no sign now of the archaeological dig which had led to her body (was it a body? Rita thought probably not, more likely a collection of bones) being discovered. She knew from the University website that they had packed up a week ago; they were working on their actual historical findings, and would post their reports in due course. There was also no sign of any police presence. Presumably they felt the events were too long ago for there to be evidence remaining at the site, or for it to be worthwhile trying to jog people's memories like they did on Crimewatch. Rita recalls the heart-rending reconstruction of events in Portugal when that little girl had been abducted; her family had taken an interest since the parents lived locally, in Glenfield, and the disappearance had been extensively covered in the local as well as the national news. There was a lot less publicity about Claire Watson, not surprisingly, 40 years on; how long would it be before her case would be filed and forgotten altogether?

* * *

"So you bought the house from Thomas and Gerald Watson?" Rita recalls this was the first question the police had asked her parents when they came back by appointment, to talk to Padma and Jahi when they got in from work (Good job they can record the Great British Bake Off thought Rita, her mother would hate to miss her favourite programme and she has a soft spot for a contestant called Brendan). It was the woman Rita had seen before, and a different man in uniform. (Rita realised, when she looked at the uniformed man, that the one on Friday must have been white while this one was black.) The woman had short, blonde hair and bright lipstick – Rita thought her hair colour was probably not natural in view of the extent of the lines on her face. The man had steady, brown, unreadable eyes.

Her parents were at the table, sitting opposite the police officers, rather like a scene from a TV cop show Rita thought. She tried to fill the kettle quietly in order to both make tea as commissioned and hear what was being said ("We have Lap Sang, or there's ordinary tea in tea bags but we only have decaffeinated" Padma had explained; the officers opted for the latter).

"And the purchase was in," both officers were looking at their notes, "1995" Rita's father interjected, "That's the year... But I don't see how we can help you." He added after a pause, wishing to be polite, "Officer" (From upstairs came a sound like a howling wolf. The officers looked startled. Padma hastily explained, "Oh, sorry, that's our son, he started doing that when he was watching the Paralympics; something to do with one of participants.").

The policewoman coughed sceptically but carried on "We're trying to trace the gentlemen, but we're not sure of their whereabouts."

"Don't their solicitors know? Or there must be other family?"

"I can't say too much as a lot of information is private to them, of course, but we have tried those avenues without success so far. There seems to be no record for the brothers other than this address in 1995 which of course is on the sale deed to you. They had an aunt but she has died. It's possible they took the money from the sale and used it to move away altogether." The woman officer paused. "Can I ask; was the house like this when you bought it?" she asked, looking round the kitchen like an admiring potential buyer.

"Now, look here," Rita's father was leaning forward now, his puzzlement turning to alarm. "You aren't going to dig up the garden are you? My lovely flower beds? You're not thinking there are more bodies?"

"No, no" the woman fanned out her hands to reassure, like a politician trying to mollify a television interviewer, "We're just trying to get a feel for where Claire lived, what the set-up was, on the day she left, that is, the last day she was seen."

"And that was?" as ever, Rita's mother was looking for facts.

"February 1972, the 12th to be precise."

"Well how could we know anything about it?" Jahi, this time.

"Yes, I appreciate there's no direct connection and a lot of time passed between 1972 and when you bought..."

"23 years!" Padma pointed out.

"...But at this stage we have very little to go on." The woman's eyes were pleading for help now, "So if you'll indulge me, what was the house like when you bought it – if you can remember?"

This should be interesting thought Rita, carefully placing on the table the tray of tea she had made and quietly going to sit on the sofa, hoping she could evade notice. Unknown to Jahi and Padma, Rita has already started her own investigations. After the first police visit she accessed a site where she could get birth, marriage and death certificates, if she had enough information. Then she had begged Mohal to take her to the library with him at the weekend. Reluctantly he had driven her to the City Centre, where he parked in a rather undesirable looking back street beside a building site, and they walked together to the library in Bishop Street, on Town Hall Square; with its high ceilings, wide corridors and arched doorways it was a reminder of grandeur from the past. Rita did not use the Central Library and was unfamiliar with the whereabouts of the computers or how to get the newspaper archives she wanted. In between helping customers with their IT queries (some of them just can't remember their passwords, he whispered to his sister), and assisting those who struggled to check out their own books, Mohal had helped her find material where she could glean background about Claire Watson's disappearance.

What was the house like when Mum and Dad moved in, before she was born? Rita was thinking.

"Well," Rita's father looked nervously at her mother, this was really her department, "As far as I can remember..." he tried.

"It was a 3 bedroom house" Padma was getting into her stride, all her grand projects dancing before her mind's eye. "A bedroom at the top of the stairs, two larger rooms, a separate WC and a bathroom. And two rooms and a small kitchen downstairs." She placed emphasis on the word 'small' to draw attention to how extensive the kitchen now was. "So first we put in a garage and put a bedroom over it, then we put in the en-suites and made the family bathroom. Then we knocked through the two downstairs rooms to make a family room and a study and finally..."

This was starting to sound like one of those home make-over programmes on TV, Rita thought, catching the police officers exchanging raised eyebrows of amusement as they helped themselves to digestive biscuits.

"Finally, we extended the back of the house to make this lovely family kitchen." Padma sat back, gesturing around the room with pride.

"Yes, this is great." The police woman graciously observed, taking in the appliances, the island, the sofa on which Rita was quietly sipping her tea, and the view of the garden.

"So the garden would have been larger?"

"Yes, it was quite overgrown." This was more Jahi's area of expertise. "The old man who lived here before – the father of the Watsons who sold to us- and of the girl I suppose - was not fit enough to do much gardening, I guess."

"And there was access down the side of the house at that time – 1995 - before you put in the garage?"

"Yes. There was just an open space. You could walk through a door there," Jahi was pointing to the spot occupied by the flat screen television, "and be outside. I think perhaps they used the space to park their car at some point. The front of the house was a garden then, also very neglected. We covered that over so there's room for our car and Mohal's, that's our son, I think you met him before. I don't remember whether there was a car here when we looked round, but of course the old man had died by then and the brothers were selling as executors so the place had an empty feel."

"And in terms of neighbours, who was here when you moved in, do you remember?"

Good question thought Rita, even she remembered the Gregsons who were the last non-Asian family to live in this part of the street. Presumably it had been more mixed when her parents moved in, the year before she was born?

"Well" her mother again, looking at her father for confirmation as she spoke, "The Banajees were definitely at number 12 – that's next door that side," she pointed to the right of the house as it faces the street, "they are older than us. All their children have grown up and are married now." Was that a wistful sigh she gave? "Next door that side," she pointed to number 8, "were a couple called Mr and Mrs Gregson. They got quite elderly and moved out, I would think, in about 2005. The Shahs and the Mehtas moved in after us – they live at 5 and 7," she indicated across the street. "But presumably you can find all this out from the Land Registry?"

"Yes, of course," said the police man, who had now devoured two more digestive biscuits. "It just helps us to get a bit of a picture. As far as we can tell, between 1972 – when Claire was last seen- and 1995, very few houses changed hands, then there was a rush of sales. A lot of older people moved out to the villages I think."

Before the police left, Rita had plucked up courage to ask them how they were sure the body – or whatever it was – belonged to Claire Watson? "Oh, we are sure of that." the woman told her, "Her brothers contacted the police in 1990 - before that they all thought she had run away and did not want to be found - but when her mother was ill, and she still couldn't be traced, they became concerned and gave DNA samples in case anything untoward had happened." ("DNA was invented in Leicester!" Nayan said when he heard this later, Jahi had to explain to him that University scientists had indeed discovered it, but did not invent, it.) "We might not have been able to make the match if she'd been found then, in 1990, but technology has come on since and we are sure. It just a shame we can't find the brothers now! Then perhaps we could try to piece together what happened."

* * *

Rita, still sitting in the back of the Peugeot, has her recall of the police visit interrupted when a football runs towards the car. "Mohal, be careful!" Rita yells and, sure enough, the path of the ball is followed by a boy of 6 or 7 years of age whose eyes are fastened on the ball and who has not seen the car. Mohal steps on the brakes and the car stops abruptly. The girls are thrown forward briefly, their multiple bracelets jangling along their arms, but as the car was not doing any speed there is no significant jolt. "Jack!", a voice is shouting and an older woman appears – too old to be Jack's mother? It was hard to tell these days – she has flabby sunburnt legs which are rather too visible under a short skirt; she has flip-flops on her feet which inhibit her running after the boy. "Come here and give me the ball!" She collects the elusive Jack and his football and heads back across the car park, not stopping to apologise or thank them for stopping.

The three of them have never been to Bradgate Park before, not even Priya who now lives so close. Parks and country walks generally did not figure on the agenda for either of their families as weekend activities. Most of their free time was spent indoors, either at home or in shopping, usually with other members of the family or 'trusted' friends. ("Well you read so much about gangs these days." Priya's mother would say. Rita's parents were also exercised that their children should not be tempted to go down the path of 'those hooligans' who had taken part in the riots and looting in town centres last year.) They were all encouraged to come home straight after school and get on with any homework or household chores waiting for them.

"Told you this was a bad idea." says Mohal.

"I just wanted to see where it happened." Rita replies, "And we won't get a better chance."

Priya, rolling her large brown eyes at this, is not sure about the use of 'we' - only Rita is really interested, although Priya has to admit she was glad of the excuse to escape her sister's wedding for an hour or so. There was a limit to how long you could spend with your sister the centre of attention and your parents glowing with pride in front of their guests.

The wedding had started at 10 and was being held in a marquee attached to a community centre in Loughborough, where Priya and her family now live, having moved from Aylestone Road some 4 years ago. Priya's mother said "It was the best move we ever made." largely because it had led to her parents introducing Meera to Jai, a lecturer at Loughborough University. After the excitement of their engagement and much discussion, argument, planning, tears and smiles among both families, the wedding ceremony had taken place that morning in front of 300 guests, including relatives from as far afield as Yorkshire, the West Midlands and London, who were still partying and partaking of the excellent buffet.

As Mohal steers his car to take them all back towards

Loughborough before they are missed, Priya glances across at her friend who is lost in thought, looking out of the window. Rita is recalling the luminous pair, going through the handing over of the bride and the ceremonious steps to show their aspirations for their life together. How happy Meera and Jai looked! Some of the words they spoke were echoing in her head." I am the sky, you are the earth… I am the thought, you are the speech… I am the ocean, you are the shore… Let us lead a joyful life of a hundred years."

A hundred years! Lady Jane Grey's marriage would not have been very long or such a joyful occasion, Rita thinks, recalling from first year history lessons that Jane's parents had had dynastic ambitions for her. The girl who was married and executed at seventeen years old had not led a joyful life, let alone for a hundred years, 'What about Claire?' Rita thinks. Was her short life joyful?

They pass a bus stop on their way back. From what the police had told her parents this was probably how Claire got there the day that she was last seen. The article she had read in the Leicester Mercury (the local evening paper) said the police had interviewed a bus conductor, who thought he remembered Claire, but that was in 1990 – a long time after her disappearance - what had prompted an investigation then? Rita pictures the girl walking from the bus stop, turning into the car park like they had done, except that then the place must have been deserted, it being February, and not the teeming torrent of humanity it currently was. Why did Claire come here? Who had she encountered? A random stranger? Someone she knew? Why leave the security and warmth of 10 Elm Drive to come all the way over here on what was probably a cold and gloomy day?

Chapter

4

"All their sport in the park is but a shadow to that pleasure that I find in Plato; alas good folk, they never felt what true pleasure meant."

Lady Jane Grey

9th *January 1972*

It was a Sunday. There was nothing to do. All the shops were shut and there no regular buses. They had eaten a desultory dry lunch of beef, over-boiled potatoes and under-cooked rice pudding. This meal was taken in silence as her parents were not talking (again) and the twins, Thomas and Gerald, on these occasions used their own system to communicate with each other in sign language. Claire now sat on her bed in her cramped room and tried to do some French revision. The mocks were next week and there seemed to be too much to cover! It was so cold (her father would not allow any heating until 5pm in winter and none at all in the summer) that she was wearing several jumpers and her gloves. She could see her breath escaping in a white cloud as she practised vocabulary out loud.

She looked at her exercise books and laughed at the pictures she had drawn in her first and second years at secondary school. There were sketches of people, a market stall bearing fruit and vegetables, and a class room, to illustrate words relating to clothes and parts of the body, food and school. There were cartoon-like pictures to show how the past tense worked. She realised as she looked at them how much better her drawing had become since Mr Clarke had been her art teacher. But back to the vocab-

"Je voudrais..." What would she like? Not cherries or strawberries or a pair of socks, that's for sure. Je voudrais… another life, please. One where her parents did not punish each other by refusing to speak to anyone. Je voudrais a decent brother or sister who would be nice to me and maybe play some board games, like the games she played with Lynn and her sister; she liked to go to Lynn's house to play Monopoly or Cluedo. They would laugh together and tease each other without fear of someone storming out or dissolving into a long silence. What was more, Lynn's mum knew what Art College was and even knew people who had been there.

Her mum and dad had only recently said anything about the parents' evening they had attended at her school before Christmas. Even then it came out as a rebuke – "Well I don't think you're amazing, whatever that Mr Clarke says." This from her father in the middle of a tirade because she was half an hour late home – 10.30 instead of 10 - which she blamed on the bus. (So Mr Clarke thought she was amazing?!)

* * *

At the time, when Mr Clarke made this statement, all Phil could say was "Claire?" and then "She's good at art?" expressed incredulously and rather contemptuously.

"Oh yes." Mr Clarke was warming to his theme, "There's no reason why she can't get a good O-level in it. She should stay and do A-level too." The look of disgust on Phil's face should have warned Mr Clarke that the door he was metaphorically pushing at was closed.

"She's the only girl who seems to grasp what I'm saying. Do you see what I mean?"

Phil and Mel weren't sure they did and neither was comfortable with the level of enthusiasm, for his subject and for their daughter, which Mr Clarke was displaying. Was this energetic approach a good idea around girls at what could only be described as 'at a difficult age' - somewhere between children and women? Phil could not remember his teachers speaking so openly and freely; they had mostly been army-trained, some had seen action in one world war or another, or, if not affected by military action they had suffered privation through rationing or evacuation or both. All of those experiences seemed to give them – as far as he could recall - a rather stiff-necked, 'grin and bear it', 'chin up laddy' attitude that brooked no nonsense and in particular practised a fervent disregard for what the pupil himself thought he wanted to do, the pupil by definition being the least qualified to know, in their opinion.

"Lovely girl" Mr Clarke was continuing his eulogy. "So pretty as well." He really was not picking up the warning signs from Phil, "In fact, I'm painting a portrait of her at the moment." Shaken from his recall of his own education, Phil started to stand up, "What do you mean by 'a portrait'?" he asked suspiciously, this did not sound right to him, 16 year old girls did not get their portraits painted!

"What kind of portrait?" Sitting in the art room surrounded by paintings of people in contemporary, in his view rather unattractive, styles was unnerving him, not to mention the shelves of papier-mâché animal masks which Mr Clarke was overseeing for the school production of Noyes Fludd, and which Phil found rather frightening and intimidating.

"Oh, don't worry." Mr Clarke had realised he needed to be placatory. "Just a head and shoulders from when she was sitting with the others in the art room. I'll show you if you like."

Phil sat back into his chair. Mel looked perplexed. What could the man be thinking of? As she puzzled more over this, nothing good came to mind and her expression changed to one of concern. Crossing back to the table where they were sitting, Mr Clarke proudly produced his work for their perusal. Phil and Mel scanned the surface sceptically, like valuers assessing authenticity.

Was it Claire? (yes).

Was it respectable? (yes).

Was it any good (neither of them was sure, neither offered an opinion).

"Alright." Was all that Phil could manage, in a voice that conveyed to Mr Clarke that the painting was only just permissible.

"But what would be the point of an O or A-level?" was the next thing Claire's father said.

* * *

At the time of this discussion, Claire was at home, and as it was a Monday she was in the back room watching Alias Smith and Jones on television. Her friend Lynn was there too – her parents had dropped her off on the way to the parents' evening - while the boys, Tom and Gerry, 10 years younger than Claire, slept upstairs. Lynn had brought apple juice and chocolate digestives – a great treat!

The television was squashed into a corner by the fireplace, the walls above it covered in brick-effect wallpaper; the fireplace was occupied by an electric fire her father had acquired in a closing down sale – "not that it'll be any use if those miners go on strike" Melanie had observed. The other 3 walls of the back room in which they were sitting were covered in wood chip paper which had been cream when painted but was now yellowing under the onslaught of Claire's parents' nicotine; her mother smoked at least 30 a day and Phil was almost as bad; in the winter months they did so mostly in the back room.

"I think the dark one is lovely." Claire said, referring to the idealised cow boys starring in the programme, "I don't know why you prefer the fair haired one."

"It's a good job you don't like him, he's mine!" replied Lynn pragmatically.

"I hope our parents don't get back before it finishes." Claire said; she was enjoying herself.

"Don't suppose they will." Her friend said. "Mine aren't seeing Mr Clarke until ten to nine and you know how he goes on!"

"There's no reason why you can't get an O-level!" In unison both girls mimicked the teacher's voice.

"Well that may be true for you," Lynn went on, adding, "Teacher's pet!"

"Shush!" Claire changed the subject, "They're about to blow open the safe!" The girls' attention returned to the screen.

* * *

That night, when her parents returned from the evening at her school, Claire went up to bed as soon as her mother had waived goodbye to the disappearing car containing Lynn and her mum and dad. She sensed her parents were having another of their long silences and in any event there was something she wanted to do before she fell asleep. Changing quickly into her pyjamas because of the cold –"soon be doing that by candlelight too!" Melanie had said, referring to the threat of a mine workers' strike which was constantly in the news; if their dispute was not resolved and the strike happened then power cuts were likely. Melanie had bought some candles in case they were needed.

Claire wriggled under the sheet and blankets - her mother made the beds so tightly you felt like a butterfly trying to become a chrysalis again - until her feet found the hot water bottle she had put in earlier. Then, leaning over the side of the bed and reaching under it, she pulled out her jewellery box. There was not much jewellery in the box, just a metal medallion her aunt Elaine had acquired for her at a jewellery party, some old plastic beads, a couple of brooches she never wore and the bangle she got for being a bridesmaid when she was 6. Underneath the tray containing these treasures were some letters. These she tenderly took out and unfolded, holding them against her heart before reading them for the umpteenth time.

As she was folding the letters and putting them back in the box she heard her parents coming upstairs, followed by the familiar sounds of their bedtime routines and bathroom ablutions. One would change while the other cleaned their teeth, then they would swap. That way neither had to speak. When all was done she would hear the click of the cord which operated the light above their bed in the room adjoining hers. She wriggled down the bed some more to get the most benefit from the covers and the water bottle. All she could see behind her closed eyes were the words he had written, "have to be with you…go away together…Art College…Paris…" and then she was asleep.

Chapter

5

"God grant you all your desires and accept my own hearty thanks for all your attention to me. Although indeed, those attentions have tried me more than death can now terrify me."

Lady Jane Grey to her executioner.

23rd September 2012

"Found anything yet?" Rita is standing at the top of the spiral staircase, staring upwards. Jahi, who would prefer to be catching up on paperwork for the surgery on a Sunday afternoon, is in the attic, having climbed the retracting steps, the only improvement, apart from some new boards, that they have made to the loft since they bought the house. He casually mentioned last week that he thought he remembered there was something left in the loft when they moved in. From memory, he'd moved the papers, or whatever they were, to one side when they'd put their own things in. From the moment he gave voice to this thought he regretted it - not only would Rita not leave the subject alone until he looked, but he was in danger of drawing Padma's attention to the loft and instigating another of her grand projects - although the loft has steep sides in view of the design of the roof, even Jahi can see it might be transformed into a useful space with some Velux windows… Those TV make-over programmes had a lot to answer for! They had taken Mohal to Hatfield the previous day, ready for fresher's week at the University, and with the extra expense of his accommodation they could do without spending more on the house, he thinks. Gingerly stepping on the wooden boards, Jahi reaches the corner he has in mind.

Standing beneath the gaping loft entrance, Rita hears a muffled exclamation – has her father bumped his head or tripped over something? Jahi's head appears at the top of the ladder, triumph shining in his face - it is good to be right! Rita watches him descend the steps with one hand on the railing, the other clutching a rather thin, disappointing, file or parcel, she can't quite tell.

"That's what I was thinking of." he smiles as he hands the bundle over to Rita in order to slide the loft steps back into place, He is pleased to have accomplished this mission while Padma is out shopping, as well as having satisfied the curiosity of his daughter.

"Now can I get on with the surgery records please?" he asks.

* * *

At school the next day Rita and Priya are in the computer area during a study period. Now they are in the sixth form they have 'free' time between lessons ("Don't call it that." says Padma. "It's time for you to use for private study. To get used to what it's like to study on your own like you will have to at uni." Two years of nagging Mohal through sixth form have taught her a lot).

"Sources and voices, thoughts and practices." They are mimicking the history teacher, Mr Thatcher. "RSVP! Remember - Sources, Voices, Practices!" Mr Thatcher's efforts at the white board have not been in vain. The point of the extra essays he wants from them (one a month until the end of term. The first is due in next week!) is to improve their skills at identifying and questioning the origin of the material they are using (who said it, when, what was their point of view or motive?) and the character and nature of the people they are studying (what were their knowledge and beliefs, what were the ideas and religion of the society they were living in?)

"Mr Thatcher's too keen." Rita says, looking at a YouTube clip of a singing dog that reminds her of Uggie, the dog in the film The Artist, which she had seen and now had on DVD, she liked it so much.

"Especially now I have my investigation to do." Rita adds.

Priya rolls her large eyes at her friend.

"Any news?" she obliges.

Rita says the police were in touch last night to say they had traced Claire's brothers to Australia. Jahi has the contact details. He told the inspector about the scrap book and she said they would call in to look at it, but that in all likelihood Jahi could give it to the brothers. ("Not exactly CSI is it?" was Mohal's response when Rita had told him this on the phone.)

"Scrap book?" queries Priya.

"Oh didn't I tell you?" Rita turns to her friend.

Priya gets out her comb ready for a long story.

* * *

While Jahi was in the study with his accounts, Rita had placed the treasure trove from the loft over the white kitchen table. She had covered the table with a plastic cloth as Padma would go ballistic if the papers left a stain. What had she got?

It was a scrap book, with some photos and postcards in it; some of them were stuck in and others had fallen loose against the staples in the middle. The scrap book had been given a paper cover; it looked like wall paper, it had an effect like brickwork and was fastened to the book with Sellotape which had dried out with age and came away at the touch, reminding Rita of dried leaves. She turned the pages of the scrap book slowly, feeling she should be wearing white gloves like those celebrities in 'Who Do You Think You Are?' "Who do you think you are, Claire?" she said quietly to herself.

What would the scrap book tell her about Claire's life? For a quick glance at the contents had convinced Rita that Claire was its creator.

The photos and postcards had been put into the book with white plastic corners which Rita had not seen before; it looked like the corners had been carefully placed so the pictures could be fitted into them. Rather a lot of bother when there were albums to slip photos in, like her Aunt Jaina did or, better still, photos could be stored digitally. She and Priya share their photos on Facebook.

The first pages contained two small, square, monochrome photographs of a white couple in the 1950s (she thought, judging by their appearance, the woman had a print dress and carried a box-like handbag on her wrist; the man had a very short haircut like the singers in the Jersey Boys, which Padma had taken her to see). The couple were near a beach. These photos were followed by several of a baby with a large forehead - or was that because she had little hair? - and eyes. The baby – Rita thought it must be Claire - was posed on a rug in one picture and, in another, sitting on the lap of a severe looking elderly woman who wore a heavy coat, and a hat and had round-rimmed glasses on her nose. Then there was a snap of a toddler running towards the camera with a glamorous looking young woman ('They knew how to do glamour in those days didn't they?' Rita thought, recalling films of the fifties she has seen). The woman is running behind the child, smiling. Rita thought, this is the woman from the earlier seaside pictures - Claire's mother? The one who died in 1990? Rita reached for her iPad to check her notes. Oh yes, from the copy of the birth certificate Rita had obtained, her mother's name was Melanie; she also had her death certificate – some sort of cancer.

On the next page, the toddler had turned into a girl (6 or 7 years old?). In one of the black and white photos she was lying on her stomach on a wooden toboggan which looked home-made, and behind her the snow lay very deep. (Rita checked her notes. Claire was 16 when she disappeared; her birth certificate said she was born on 29 September 1955. So this was winter 1962 or 1963?) In the next picture, the girl was grinning, with her two top front teeth missing, and standing in front of a Christmas tree.

Over the page, the black and white squares had changed to larger, rectangular pictures, in colour. One was of the same girl - you could tell by the eyes - who was sitting on a sofa with a baby either side of her. So this was Claire Watson with her brothers! They were born in, what, 1966? Powers of deduction were not needed for this, however, as in a large and clear hand Claire (or someone?) had written under these photos. The style of the writing reminded Rita of the writing in prizes at school or on the place names at the VIP tables at Meera's wedding.

The presence of the writing made the absence of some of the photos more poignant. There was a gap – like those missing teeth in the Christmas picture - where 'Claire's first day at senior school' should be for example, and an empty space for 'Claire on Sunday School outing' (Sunday School? Rita was not sure what that was. Maybe Claire had extra tutoring like Rita's cousins do?) The babies are labelled Thomas and Gerald. Rita knew from her cousins that although they were called identical twins, the family would know which is which; Rita never muddled Shreya with Shona, These must be the brothers from whom Mum and Dad had bought the house.

The next page had Claire on an old-fashioned looking bike (like something out of Miss Marple, Rita thinks) she was wearing, as far as Rita could tell, plimsolls on her feet, trousers with loops on the end of the legs and a white Airtex Tee shirt. Her hair was fair – obviously natural and not from a bottle like the police woman's - and scooped into a pony tail. She had no fringe and her hairstyle made her forehead look prominent. She was standing by the pedals, not in motion, and in the foreground of the picture were two small boys on scooters. They wore baggy shorts from which their legs emerged like sticks of pink rock. Their shoes were like girls' sandals, Rita thought, and they were very scuffed. The children were in a garden which Rita could just about identify as the garden of her house. Where there was now a six foot wooden fence there were just rows of wire between posts so that you could see into the garden next door. A few bushes had been planted in the bed along the border but these had not grown very high. Most of the garden was grass; there were no raised beds, water feature, decking or summer house – all these were Jahi's creations.

Rita noticed that on this page, instead of the large formal black writing, the years were written on the pages in a smaller script, and in blue ink around which someone had drawn small depictions of flowers and trees – they were good pictures Rita thought. This one said '1970'. Over the page there were more gaps; these were all titled 1971 - 'Family holiday', and 'November'; and then 'Christmas'.

Among the loose pictures, which had fallen into the folds at the centre of the scrapbook , was one of two boys riding on donkeys on a beach, with Claire (as Rita now thought of her) standing between them. She had on a white broad-brimmed sun hat; she looked sunburnt on her bare arms and neck. She was not so much smiling at the camera as glaring at it, Rita thought, as if she wished it would go away.

Another photo showed Claire standing against a fireplace holding a painting. Rita peered closely at the scene, amused to see the wall paper in the background was the same as the paper which had been used to cover the book she was examining, and was amazed to see the painting was a portrait of a girl who must be Claire herself. Who could have done that, she wondered?

As Rita finishes her description of the scrap book she notices she has a text message from her father on her phone, which is on 'silent' to avoid confiscation.

"Oh," she tells Priya, "Dad says the police have looked at the scrapbook and say we can give it to Claire's brothers. They already have photos of her – the ones they used in 1990 when they tried to trace her." She sounds disappointed; she was hoping it might hold a vital clue.

Rita clicks on to the Bradgate website to put herself into the frame of mind of Lady Jane Grey and her family, who are the subject of her first additional essay. "What's your essay about?" she asks Priya absentmindedly while she mulls over the exact approach for her own.

"That's easy," comes the reply, "Rasputin."

"As in that old Bony M song?" Rita asks.

"The very same."

"Lover of the Russian Queen?" Rita quotes the lyrics.

"Well, that's what the song says, yeh," says Priya, "And that's the point." She picks up some extracts she has printed off already. "It's a good story – a monk who gets too close to the Royal family and has too much influence through his apparent ability to 'cure' their son of his haemophilia. But it says here that everything you read about him has to be taken sceptically."

"Mmnnh" Rita is only half listening.

"Well I'm finding out a lot about Ra- Ra- Rasputin." Priya continues. "It seems to me the other people at court were jealous and resented Rasputin, then of course there was the revolution and there was no one to defend his reputation." Priya pauses, seeing that her friend is still distracted, "So have you settled on an approach to yours yet?"

"Not quite." Rita is still thinking. "Yours was easy. You're thinking of those lovely outfits Keira Knightley wore in that film, Anna Karenina." She teases. "I guess Rasputin and the Queen is a bit like the stories about Queen Victoria and that Scotsman, the one played by Billy Connolly in the film."

"John Brown." Priya supplies.

"Hmmn. Seems like if you have power other people resent it or want to influence you, or else they distrust those around you who seem to have your ear." Rita concludes.

"Guess that's why we have to question the sources. What is the evidence and where is it coming from?" Priya agrees.

* * *

Rita and Jahi wait until Friday as their call will have to be late in the evening (11 pm in Leicester, 10 am in Canberra). Looking at the twin brothers of Claire on Skype, Rita thinks for a moment they must be out in a snowdrift somewhere, until she realises they are sitting on a white sofa which is situated on a white carpet. It is strange to be looking at two middle aged men who are so alike. Both have hair which is receding at the front and greying identically at the sides. Both wear glasses with little lines across the middle – bifocals Rita thinks, like Mr Thatcher wears. She recalls when he first got them; he seemed to be staring at the wrong person when he asked a question until he got used to the lenses.

The female police inspector has put the families in touch (Might as well, Mohal had said on the phone. They can't be suspects, they were kids at the time, and she was dead long before our family took over the house, so we're not in the frame either. There was nothing to lose in his opinion. He then went on to say quite a bit about how it was a self- help society now – solve your own crimes - and more besides about the lax attitude of the police which made Rita think maybe Mohal - who had been very supportive of the police at the time of the riots the previous year - had been to meetings of disaffected groups at uni, she hoped he wasn't getting in with the wrong people already).

"Mr Patel." one of the twins says,

"And Miss Patel" says the other.

"We are Thomas,"

"And Gerald,"

"Watson" they say together. Like an old married couple they are clearly used to finishing one another's sentences.

"Pleased to meet you." says Jahi 'who says that on Skype?' thinks Rita, watching as her father instinctively gives a little bow. (OMG what will they think?)

"You live..."

"So..."

Thomas and her father begin to talk at the same time.

"Sorry" they both say, holding up their hands like batsmen who have miscalled a run. ("All in the timing, Dad," Rita thinks.)

"You are Claire's brothers?" she interjects, deciding to try to dispel the awkwardness.

"Yes that's right" says Gerald. Rita is detecting a faint Australian accent. How long have they been out there? Over fifteen years? They don't look the tanned, surfing types (although maybe they were when they were younger?) Rita thinks. She notices they have the same habit of pushing their spectacles to the bridge of their nose when they speak. Rita can also see ice cubes and slices of lemon floating in the large glasses of water the men have in front of them and from which they take sips at frequent intervals; it must be warm where they are! Rita thinks. By contrast she and her father have treated themselves to mugs of hot chocolate.

"And we live in your house now. The one you were in when your sister, Claire disappeared." Rita puts in.

"I bought it from you in 1995, after your mother died I think." Jahi asserts himself now his daughter has got the ball rolling and he is adjusting to the pace of talking to these men thousands of miles away. (Rita notes the use of 'I' silently reciting to herself that it was Padma's parents who put up most of the money for the purchase.)

"Yes," Gerald again, unwilling to contradict but anxious to get the record straight on their side, reflecting his accountant's instincts "Actually it was after our father died. Mother went first, in 1990. That was the time when we asked the police to see if they could find Claire."

"They put out an appeal on Radio 4 and everything." Thomas supplies, "But no one knew where she was or what had happened to her."

"You must be very sad at the recent developments." Jahi sympathises. "We send our condolences." There is a moment's pause while everyone gathers their thoughts.

"Yes, a sad end to our search." says Thomas "We've found her at last, but it leaves so many questions unanswered." This from Gerald.

"What have the police said?" Rita is keen to get more information if she can.

"Only that the remains in the Park are a match for Claire – we gave DNA samples in 1990 so there's no doubt."

"Why do you think she was there?" Jahi gives Rita a sharp look when she asks this. They are meant to be showing the brothers the scrapbook not interrogating them.

"We were only six years old at the time she was last seen so we didn't have much idea what was going on then." Gerald seems to want to tell their story.

"It was the Sunday before we knew anything was up."

"The 13th?" Rita is mentally consulting her timeline.

"We were in the garden having a kick-around (Jahi imagines the scene transported to his well-manicured lawns and shudders slightly; of course it all looked very different when they bought the house and must have been different again in 1972, judging by the photos in the scrapbook).

"Dad came out and said had we seen Claire?" asked Thomas.

"We didn't think anything of it, we just said no." Gerald replied.

"Then Mum came out of the back door and said 'She's gone Phil' or something like that. She looked quite shaken which was a surprise to us, it took a lot to rattle our mother."

"Dad said she couldn't be gone, what did Mum mean and she said she couldn't find her, there was no note, but her coat and bag were gone."

The men were rushing through their story now as if recalling the events might bring their sister back, or yield some meaning to the events.

"They must have called her friends? Relatives? People she might have gone to?" Rita can't work out how a 16 year old girl could just vanish.

Their mother had phoned everyone she could think of, they said, but no one had seen her. She had been frantic to call the shop where Claire was working on the Saturday but it was closed, it being Sunday, and she had no number for any of the staff, so that had to wait until Monday.

"Didn't they call the police?" asked Rita.

"Why didn't they realise until Sunday?" Jahi thinks he would know straight away if one of his children had not appeared when expected.

The brothers look at each other as if telepathically deciding who will answer which question.

"Our parents went out that Saturday night, to one of their folk song evenings. Claire should have been back to babysit us. She was due back when they went out, so we were ok. When she didn't return we just put ourselves to bed – it had happened before – we didn't want to get her into trouble by saying anything. Our parents assumed she was in the house when they got back."

"And the police?" Rita probes.

"As far as we know, the police weren't involved until Monday."

(The 14th, Rita thinks, two days after Claire went missing, so much for the golden hour she has heard about on Crimewatch!)

It seemed their parents only decided they needed some help after they spoke with the shop manager, who told them Claire had not turned up for work the previous Saturday. The shop had assumed she was ill and that she would be in touch. The only number they had for her was the home number and as the house was empty on the Saturday no-one answered. ('Oh glory' thinks Rita. 'No answering machine? No mobile phone? How did these people manage to do anything?')

"What was found with her?" Rita brings the men back to the present from their reminiscing.

"Her necklace was with her," Gerald nearly choking even now at the memory. "We remembered it well – it was a metal one she got for her birthday and she wore it all the time when she went out. We knew it was Claire when we saw a picture of it, even before the DNA results. Also her wrist had an old fracture, an accident she had falling on ice as a child. Our mother used to tell us about it to stop us from larking around when it was slippy underfoot."

As it had said in the paper, after all this time there had been a lot of decomposition. The police had also recovered a large key, a number of small beads and the remains of a plastic comb and a plastic handbag, Gerald added.

"The police have nothing to go on, it seems. It's not clear what happened to her. Whether it was an accident or a crime. How she came to be there at all." Thomas explains.

"I'd like to help if I can," Rita offers, ignoring her father's stare and shake of his head. "I want to know what happened to Claire. I've been looking at the old newspaper reports."

"Well any help would be welcome." says Gerald, his brother nodding beside him.

"We have something more cheerful to show you I hope" Jahi changes the direction of the conversation, seeing that the brothers are getting quite distressed. Rita holds up the scrap book so they can see it.

Two eager matching faces peer at it through the screen.

"Oh yes, that was Claire's!" exclaims Thomas.

"It was in your attic you say?" Gerald replies.

"Are there photos in it?"

The years peel away and the faces of the 50 year olds are restored to their boyish liveliness and interest.

"Photos and postcards" Rita holds up a sample page to show them.

"That's us on our scooters." Gerald.

"There's Claire, look at her pony tail!" Thomas, adding "This is marvellous. We don't have many photographs from when we were kids."

Rita turns to the last page, the holiday snap "Oh look, there we are at Cromer! That holiday with the funfair we went to on the last night!" Thomas again.

"There are postcards too" Rita tells them.

"Claire used to collect them." They tell her "Some were from friends and relatives, some were from..." they seem stuck for the phrase "Not pen friends, what is it...chain letters."

"Chain letters?" Rita is puzzled, she is not familiar with this expression.

"It's a list of people who write to each other, or send each other postcards. You add your name to the list and when it comes to the top, people write to you or send you cards. Something like that. She got cards from all the country!" Gerald explains.

('So that is why there are cards with addresses but no messages' thinks Rita.)

"Shall we post the scrap book to you?" Jahi is asking.

"No, please keep it until we get over there. It is too precious to risk losing and the post is tricky here, if you're not in when they deliver they just return it, we couldn't risk that happening." Thomas said.

"We hope we can have a funeral in about a month and we'll be over for that. We hope you both will come to it?" Gerald extends the invitation.

"How did she die do they think?" Rita is keen to add to her knowledge despite the sharp look this earns her from Jahi.

"Hard to tell after all this time but it looks like she banged the back of her head. She must have fallen – or been pushed. I just hope it was over quickly for her."

The tone is sombre now and the men look tired. Jahi decides to wrap up the conversation.

"So sorry to have to talk in these circumstances. Let us know when the funeral is."

"Good day" the twins say together.

"Good day." Rita and her father echo.

* * *

The next day, Rita is in her bedroom, half sitting and half lying on her pink duvet cover, the various cushions she has acquired to decorate the room are piled around her. She has Priya on loud speaker while she talks to her on her iPhone, simultaneously surfing the net, Justin Bieber playing in the background. She has filled Priya in on the conversation with Claire's brothers.

"Any more ideas about your first extra essay?" Priya asks her friend.

"Oh yes," replies Rita, hitting the keys of her lap top with a possible title as she talks to her friend – "Frances Brandon, good or bad?" she says as she writes.

"Frances Brandon?" says Priya, "Who's he?"

"Not he, silly." Rita giggles, "It's a she-Lady Jane Grey's mother."

Priya shrugs her shoulders but light is dawning as she

recalls the Park they visited on the day of her sister's wedding; her mother had not been pleased to see the three of them sneaking back to the gathering. ("Where have you been?" she had hissed, "You need to support your sister today of all days.")

Rita explains patiently. "It's not really about Lady Jane Grey at all, but how much she was controlled by her mother. Frances Brandon. Well Frances Grey she became when she married Jane's father, has been painted as ambitious and scheming; she was accused of being cruel, beating Jane and forcing her daughter to offer herself as Queen."

"Sounds like she deserved whatever karma was coming to her. What goes around comes around." says Priya philosophically.

"Well that's partly it. She ended up ok, while Jane, her husband and her father were executed, all of which suggests they didn't think so badly of her at the time. Most of the criticism is by later historians and writers. I can argue the evidence for her as an evil schemer does not stack up."

"So where did the idea come from?"

"Well, there's one historian who says the family quarrelled a bit about the marriage, but the rest is conjecture by later commentators. Queen Mary did not punish her, and in fact Jane's sisters were bridesmaids at her wedding. Frances married again, after Jane's father was executed; again, some writers say he was a groom – so below her socially - and younger than her; all a bit 'Hello' magazine really. But none of that is quite true and when she died she was buried in Westminster Abbey. Hardly where you would put a traitor. Apparently her second husband put on the tomb "true worth alone survives the tomb.""

"Wow, strong stuff." Priya is impressed.

"Yes, I think they were making a point." said Rita.

"So remind me - how did Jane get to be the 9 day Queen then? From a place in Leicester?" Priya's tone is sceptical.

"Well, Bradgate was a medieval deer park of course, that's why there are still so many deer around in there. Frances was born at Hatfield House. You remember we went there on a history trip in year 8?"

"Hatfield, where Mohal is going to Uni?" Priya's interest is aroused now.

"Yes, remember now? There were two houses there when we went – the Old Palace, which would have been the one where Frances was born, and the big house you go round today which was built a bit later. Then Frances married John Grey who was from round here – Groby - his father had started to build a mansion in Bradgate Park; it was probably once like the house at Hatfield, but it's ruins now. Quite eerie from what you can see on the website – imagine the ruins at night! Like something from Twilight" Rita refers to the film all the girls at school are crazy for.

"I was hoping we might see it from the car when we went the other day, but we were too far away. We should go back and look."

"I suppose." Priya is less sure; would her mother allow that?

"Jane Grey was born in that house. Incidentally, she wasn't Frances's first baby. She lost two before her."

"So sad. But quite common then I suppose." Priya interjects. "Jane had sisters you said?"

"Yes, that's right, Catherine and Mary, The family were protestants. Jane was some sort of cousin to Elizabeth the First and a grandchild of Henry VIII's sister. When she was 10 Jane went with Elizabeth to live with Catherine Parr, Henry's last wife, who was also a protestant. Anyway, when Edward VI died young, the Protestants thought it was worth a try – to put Jane on the throne in preference to Mary, Henry's daughter, who was Catholic. The Duke of Northumberland had been the Lord Protector under Edward. He got Jane to marry his son, called – strangely - Guildford!"

Both girls find this name odd and giggle.

"So Northumberland was more likely putting pressure on everyone I think. And Jane's father was probably ambitious too, and then he changed sides when he realised it wasn't going to work. He quickly declared for Mary and abandoned Jane." Rita sounds disapproving.

"Charming!" Priya chimes in.

"Jane and her husband were sentenced to death for treason but it wasn't carried out straight away. The pair might have got off I think except that her father joined another rebellion, so then all 3 got executed. At the scaffold, Jane said she had never sought the throne but merely accepted it."

"All to avoid having a Catholic as Queen!" says Priya

"Yes. Strange where beliefs can lead you." Rita adds "Jane and Frances were both in the wrong place at the wrong time if you ask me." she says then "Oh look!"

Rita is logged on to the website for the University archaeology team. There is a page reporting on their latest digs in the Bradgate area, with pictures of the rolling expanse of green-grey grassland and clumps of trees which make up the Park, together with the eighteenth century folly, which looks like a giant coffee mug, built 700 feet above sea level and visible for several miles across the County.

"They found a brooch in the Park, an Anglo Saxon one, and a necklace. Maybe someone hid them there, or maybe they dropped them. Long before the deer park it used to be full of trackways, people would use the park to make their way across country, between the Roman roads, so they may have left things behind as they travelled."

"Maybe the travellers were in a hurry – had to move quickly. It can't have been very safe in those days, no police." says Priya, "Is that all they found?"

"Yes" says Rita. "Just the brooch and necklace and a few coins; nothing to indicate a settlement there; nothing like a temple or a well or anything. The sites nearer Markfield were more productive."

"Not much to show for it then" says Priya, "Spooky that if they hadn't dug there they'd never have found Claire and her whereabouts would have remained a mystery."

"Life's a Mystery" Rita says, repeating a favourite phrase of Padma's.

She adds, "I'll tell you something else that's spooky. The date that Lady Jane Grey was executed, and the date that Claire Watson was last seen is the same, 12th February!"

Chapter

6

"Although it hath pleased God to hasten my death by you, by whom my life should rather have been lengthened, yet can I patiently take it, that I yield God more hearty thanks for shortening my woeful days."

Lady Jane Grey

18th December 1971

The shoe shop closed as usual at 5.30pm and by 6pm the assistants had tidied up, put on their coats and gloves and were filing out, talking about their plans for the evening. Claire always thought there was something reassuring about walking out of the shop at night. All the shoes were reunited with their pairs, resettled back into their boxes and the boxes were back on the correct shelves. The darkness was brightened by the Christmas decorations strung across Charles Street and Gallowtree Gate, so that as the shop lights were switched off behind them the darkness did not envelop them but they were left in a glow of lights, like the glow from a fire.

It had been a very busy day, the run up to Christmas always was according to Ian, the senior assistant. Claire worked on the top floor with ladies shoes. From there, if you got a chance to glance outside, the view was over Charles Street and so high up the throngs of shoppers looked like insects swarming and the buses looked like toys. People accessed the ladies department by means of an elegant wooden staircase which must have been there since the shop was built in the last century - a test for the shoes the customers were wearing, especially the current fashion for platform heels and soles.

That day the most common request was for slippers as presents for relatives and it was easy to show the range and let the buyer choose. The slippers could be exchanged if they kept the receipt. The more difficult customers were the ladies wanting party shoes. Claire fetched them boxes of black patent shoes, keeping a polite smile on her face, trying to keep track of where each box and pair were and where to replace them- like a giant game of Memory - order was everything in the smooth running of the shoe shop and if she was to avoid Ian's wrath.

The best sale she had that day had been 3 pairs of sling backs to the same customer. An Asian man had climbed the stairs followed by three ladies wearing saris under their winter coats. Claire had no idea who or what age they were – could they be his mother? His sister? His wives? (They could have more than one wife, couldn't they?) The man had chosen the style and they had tried on the appropriate sizes. Claire never found out whether the women spoke English, as the man did all the talking to her, the women talking among themselves quietly in a language Claire did not understand, although she had heard similar tones around the town centre.

"Goodbye Claire."

"Evening Alex."

The other assistants were heading off to catch their buses. Ian, as senior sales assistant, was the last to leave, setting the alarm and locking the door behind him. He had a car, a Mini, which he had parked on the outskirts of town near the St Matthews estate, so he strode off in that direction.

Claire and Alex stood a little nervously together, then turned in the opposite direction to the others. Alex shyly picked up Claire's hand in his. "Come on" he said and they walked together in the direction of Belvoir Street, weaving their way towards Town Hall Square. As they did so they passed shop windows adorned with tinsel and streamers, wishing customers a Happy Christmas and New Year. Other couples were promenading in the dark, wrapped up in their coats and scarves, either meandering slowly towards the Square or making their way in the opposite direction towards the Clock Tower and possibly to the pubs around Humberstone Gate, where the new Sainsbury's had opened.

When they got to the Square, Claire and Alex strolled from display to display. There were various scenes using puppets to show pantomime themes – Aladdin, Cinderella, Puss in Boots - a depiction in miniature of Santa and his reindeer, and a nativity scene. They laughed secretly together at some of the figures – "That shepherd looks like Ian!" "What's that cow doing?" Alex put his arm round Claire. both feeling the freedom of the dark and not being observed. When they had seen all the Christmas scenes they sat on a bench in the Square and exchanged Christmas presents.

"It's only something small." Claire said, although she had spent a lot of time choosing which fountain pen to give him.

"Mine too." said Alex, who had picked out a small glass hedgehog he thought Claire would like.

"I'll have to get my bus soon." Claire said. "They go mad if I'm late."

"Come on my bike" Alex was persuasive, "Then we'll have more time."

"Better not" Claire said, recalling how the man next door had seen them together before. "Too risky."

"Okay" Alex conceded. "Let's meet up after Christmas where no one will recognise us. Remember that day I took you out to Bradgate Park?"

Claire recalled the day well. It had been in November. She had asked Lynn to tell their form teacher, Mrs Masterson, that she was not feeling well (period pains) and had gone home. This was risky as the school secretary would probably ring home to inform her mother and check Claire was there. Well, she, Claire, would have to face the music if that happened. Alex picked her up round the corner from school. She climbed up behind him onto the bike and they rolled along, weaving their way through the traffic, until they reached the less busy dual carriageway and the houses gave way to a more rural landscape.

She had been to Bradgate Park before; her parents sometimes took them there for a picnic. The last time had been in the summer. The ritual was to find a place to park, which was always stressful, her father being particular about the spot they chose, and then they all climbed to 'Old John', the monument on the hill. The twins had larked around as they walked, kicking a football between them and frequently losing it in the scrub and gorse that fringed the path. Her father strolled ahead, looking back only occasionally to see if they were following, and her mother brought up the rear. At the summit, reached with a little loss of breath by all of them, was a metal disc showing what could be seen from the vantage point. Various other people were gathered round it, so they joined in briefly, Claire's father taking a photograph of them all. Then it was back down the hill for hard boiled eggs and potted meat sandwiches eaten sitting on a rug beside the car.

Reaching the perimeter with Alex, they easily found a safe spot for the motor bike and stood together by the wooden entrance gate to the car park which was virtually empty – there were just a few vehicles suggesting others had taken advantage of the dry weather to take a stroll outdoors. There was a car in the lay-by opposite and Claire was just starting to notice it was the same type as their family car – a Morris Traveller - when she was distracted by Alex leaning in towards her for a kiss. She stopped noticing her surroundings, and when she became conscious of them again, several intoxicating minutes later, the car in the lay-by had gone.

They wandered hand in hand along the bracken-edged path, meandering between trees sometimes, talking contentedly and laughing sometimes, until they reached the red brick ruins of the old house, where previous fireplaces could just be made out and old chimney breasts pointed skywards. The pair sat on a low wall for a while, peering at the deer, who seemed to be staring back at them, and trying to see if they could see the figures of anybody walking in the distance.

When she had realised the time, Claire had hastened to get back. Alex took her into the City centre but when she walked to the stop she found that her bus home was late - there had been a fire in a furniture shop which had closed all the roads apparently. Claire was worried her mother would know she had missed school, but fortunately by the time she got home it was after six and her mother had gone out to her night school class, leaving the boys alone as Phil was working late that day. The twins had had their tea and Melanie had left some shepherd's pie in the oven to keep warm for Claire and her father. Claire questioned the boys as she put them to bed as to their mother's mood and was relieved to hear she had not been particularly bad tempered that day. She had kept her fingers crossed that Melanie was unaware of her afternoon adventure.

Claire wanted to meet Alex at the park again but remembering the way her heart fluttered when she realised how late she would be and the trouble she might get into, she thought carefully for a moment before responding.

"I'd like to." she said, "Only it's difficult."

"Can't you get away in the holidays?" He suggested. "Say you are going to a friend's house."

Claire resolved to do that. It was Lynn's birthday on the 27th. She could say she was going to her house and get the bus out to the Park instead. This was the plan they made as they parted, wishing each other a happy Christmas in advance.

* * *

A week later the boys had woken early; it was Christmas day and about 5 in the morning. They had bounded in to Phil and Mel shouting

"It's Christmas day!" and

"Has it snowed?"

"Go back to bed" Phil had pleaded hoarsely. He and Mel had been up until midnight wrapping presents and tidying the front and back rooms. This was a throw-back to when Melanie's mother used to visit for Christmas. She had died when Claire was seven, so she remembered a few things about her – mostly her soft wrinkly skin, her large fur gloves and the smell of Elizabeth Arden perfume. Melanie's father having been killed in the final stages of the second world war, and Philip's parents having died in a train crash in 1951 - they had been on their way to a friend's wedding, leaving their only son, Philip, then aged 21, alone to deal with their affairs - there had been few relatives to attend the brief Registry Office wedding of Phil and Mel. Melanie's parents had not been wealthy and their estates were barely sufficient for their daughters to pay for their funerals. Philip's father had been on the board of a tyre company and his untimely death left Phil with a large lump sum which had come in useful when he and Melanie needed a house. Phil thought about his parents often – how his father worked hard to be 'comfortable' and ended up dying young. He groaned as he turned over in bed. Five hours sleep were not enough for him.

"Has Father Christmas been?" this, from Tom.

Mel sat up, rollers in her hair ('How does she sleep like that? Phil always thought. How uncomfortable!'). Her bri-nylon nightie was a washed-out colour which might once have been pink or orange but was now a pale imitation of neither.

"Go to your room or there'll be no presents!" she had barked at them. Chastened, the boys had crept away at a slower speed than that at which they had arrived. They had been tempted to knock on Claire's door to see if she was interested in the fact that it was Christmas but they knew this would only lead to more trouble and maybe their mother would implement her threat, so they had wriggled back under their sheets and blankets, taking comics with them to peruse until the official waking up time came.

From her small bedroom next door, Claire had heard the boys charging in. She knew they would get a sharp reply and heard them leaving as well. Then she had turned over and tried to get some more sleep until morning. It was so cold in her room she could see her breath in the early morning light, like a white cloud hovering. She was hoping for the Rod Stewart LP- both she and Alex liked him - for Christmas – but she was resigned to getting another collection of embroidered handkerchiefs and bath cubes. Maybe Aunty Elaine would send a record voucher which she could put towards an LP, she thought.

* * *

The family were all seated round the dining table by eight o'clock, eating toast and pork pie – a Christmas tradition from Melanie's family apparently. The Church service was at 9.30 and they needed to get there is good time as it was expected to be busy. The boys were swinging their legs excitedly under the table and eyeing the piles of presents under the tree. Claire was experienced enough to know that while some would undoubtedly contain treats and surprises, some were empty boxes which her mother liked to wrap up 'to make the tree look nice'.

"Can't we open one?" her brothers had tried.

"Just a small one?"

But the answer was an emphatic negative and they knew better than to push their luck by trying further.

When they arrived at St Andrew's the vicar was beaming, the Church was gleaming – it always got an extra scrub at Christmas- and baby Jesus was in his crib. All the children – even Tom and Gerry - sang *Away In a Manger* "You should help with the Sunday School!" Melanie hissed to Claire not for the first time; Claire just shrugged and looked ahead of her. She didn't get on with the girls who helped with Sunday School; they went to a different school to her and had different interests - like going to pop concerts; one of them was a David Bowie fan and another had even been to the Isle of Wight festival. What would Melanie say if she started putting up posters of David Bowie instead of the Partridge family or went off to the Isle of Wight?

The congregation, having absorbed the sermon on Jesus' poverty and humble beginnings, filed out proudly in their best coats and hats, queuing to shake the hand of Reverend Drake, and looking forward to the Christmas dinner to come. Some children had brought presents with them – "Lucky them!" the boys said – largely items to keep them quiet like dolls, crayons and colouring books. The new bikes and roller skates would be on display later.

The boys were banished to their room when they arrived back home. There was to be no disturbance of the front or back rooms until after Christmas dinner. This had been the way when Melanie's mother was alive and had visited for Christmas and the tradition continued, even though there was no one now to see the orderliness of it. Claire barely remembered her Granny, who had died when she was seven, but what she did recall did not tally with an ogre who had to be placated with tidy rooms.

The day crawled along like slow traffic, missing the routine that usually helped time speed by. Melanie produced a dry turkey and overcooked vegetables which she and Philip ate with a glass of sherry to show it was Christmas day. After they had washed up – Claire at the sink and the boys supposedly drying the pots but actually using their tea towels as cloaks or weapons - they opened their presents and played the new board games the boys had been given. Everyone seemed pleased with the little gifts Claire had found for them at the Guides Christmas Fair. Then it was tinned salmon sandwiches and Morecombe and Wise before the twins succumbed to slumber and Claire climbed the stairs not long after.

Hurriedly undressing in the cold and wriggling under the covers, Claire reached beneath her bed for her jewellery box, where she had placed the present from Alex. Opening it carefully in order to be as quiet as possible – she did not want her parents or her brothers to know what she was doing – she found the tiny glass face of a hedgehog looking at her. Perfect! Claire smiled. If she could just get through Boxing Day – no doubt a football-related activity for the boys – then she could see Alex again at Bradgate Park.

Chapter

7

"I do wash my hands in innocency, before God and the face of you, good Christian people this day."

Lady Jane Grey

10*th* October 2012

"So on the whole your essays weren't bad." Mr Thatcher is addressing the History Group who are gathered round him in a semi-circle. It's the last period of the day so they have brought their bags, which are crouching at their feet like loyal dogs waiting to go for a walk, and their coats are draped, some more tidily than others, over the chair backs. This rather spoils the business effect that Mr Thatcher was aiming for.

"Now, what years are you doing for Black History month and why?"

The students shuffle on their seats, trying not to be the first to speak, their eyes cast down on the ground. Mr Thatcher decides to start with one of the ends of the row (well it's been a long week and he's rather tired). One by one they recite their next essay subjects.

"1990" "because?" "Release of Nelson Mandela."

"1865" Mr Thatcher looks quizzical "Amendment for the abolition of slavery in the US."

"1968" a pause "Assassination of Martin Luther King."

"1854" "Mary Secole in the Crimea", this is Priya's topic.

"1955" "Rosa Parkes refused to give up her seat on the bus."

"1972" Mr Thatcher has been writing the years on the white board and at this he swivels round to look at Rita with a puzzled expression. Priya however is rolling her eyes. Rita's obsession continues!

"Explain?"

"Expulsion from Uganda by Idi Amin. That's when my parents came here, with their families."

* * *

When the lesson ends Rita and Priya are waiting just inside the school entrance for Priya's mum to appear; Rita is going to her house tonight.

"1972!" Priya is saying "OMG. Trust you. The year Claire disappeared."

"Well, it's interesting, innit?" Rita rejoins. "She was in my house, probably had my bedroom, although I expect it looked different then. And later the same year my parents' families came to Leicester! They didn't have a thing."

"How did they find a place to live? My grandparents were already settled here, they had been for a few years."

"The Welfare Board helped them apparently… it was set up by local people, maybe like your grandparents. There was nothing organised otherwise." Rita explains.

"Why did those families come to Leicester?" Priya asks.

"Well, as you say, some Asians from India – Hindu families especially – were already here. My father's uncle, for example. But his house was very crowded already according to my father."

"How old were your parents when they came?"

"My mother was 4, my father was 7. So he remembers a bit more than she does, but they don't talk about it much and neither did my grandparents."

"And they lived in Highfields? Like my mum and my aunty?" Priya asks as she peers out, seeking her mother's car.

"Yes. The house was very basic, Mum says, and crowded. And while they were living there, Claire was living at my house, then, with everything you could need."

"You don't know that." Priya corrects her, searching in her school bag for her comb.

"Well, I mean, a roof, food, her Dad had a job."

"Yes, what did he do?"

"Overlocker." Priya looks puzzled as Rita says this "I know, that's what's on the birth certificate I got."

"Where has my mum got to?" Priya peers into the street again, as if by looking hard enough she could conjure up her mother.

"So why was that girl on the other side of town, all the way out at Bradgate Park?" Priya indulges her friend.

"That's a key question." Rita retorts as Priya's mother's car appears. The girls load themselves in the back.

"Hello girls."

"Hiya"

Pleasantries over, the friends continue their conversation as Mrs Shah negotiates the early evening rush hour on the ring road. "Really, they did not build this road wide enough. I don't know what they were thinking." Was Mrs Shah's common complaint. Rita thinks, 'The ring road did not exist in Claire's day. A journey to another part of the City generally meant going in to the centre and out again, unless you were very familiar with the back roads.'

"Was Claire unhappy?" Priya is looking for more background "I can't imagine running away from home."

"I should hope you can't." Priya's mother joins in from the driving seat, looking at her daughter in the rear view mirror.

"If you were unhappy you should always talk to you father or me, or Meera if you must. That's what families are for." She adds reassuringly.

Priya is always asking what would happen if she married someone and then didn't like them. She knows that, like most Hindu families, hers strongly deplores the idea of divorce. To answer her concerns her mother would say "You can always come back to me and your Dad. There's always a home for you girls; but don't worry, we'll find a nice man for you."

Certainly, Meera seemed happy with the selection they had made for her.

* * *

They are on their way to the osteopath. Rita will keep Priya company while her mother has treatment for her lower back ("The trouble we women have when we have to give birth" she often says, looking pointedly at whichever of her daughters is in the room at the time). Mrs Shah finds a space to park on Uppingham Road and they walk to the entrance which is above a photocopying shop. Climbing the steep stairs – there is a lift but Priya's mother does not like using it, "I get claustrophobic." She says - they come to a reception area bathed in green and smelling slightly of mint. There is a kettle and some herbal tea bags by the reception desk, together with some magazines. The girls settle themselves down while Mrs Payne ('Great name for an osteopath!' thought Rita when she first heard it) attends to Priya's mother.

Priya picks up one of the magazines.

"They say Catherine Middleton is pregnant!" she tells Rita

"They always say that." says Rita, who opens her iPad to look at her notes for 1972.

Claire Watson was living in her house in Elm Drive. It was a 3 bedroom house then, with two rooms and a small kitchen downstairs. Priya's mother would probably find that claustrophobic too, and it sounded cramped compared to the light airy house Padma had made number 10 into. It was probably cold in the winter, they may not have had central heating, and in 1972, Rita has seen on television programmes about the seventies, there was also the miners' strike and the three day week to contend with; there were regular power cuts and people had to sit in the dark. It was hard to believe.

63

1972 was when Padma and Jahi arrived in Leicester as children with their families. Rita knows this from the occasional conversations she has overheard among her relatives. It must have seemed strange and cold to them she thinks; Rita has footage of elderly Indian women shivering, hugging coats over their saris. Many of the women had their dark hair in long plaits all the way down their backs. The boys and men were smartly dressed in suits with fashionably large collars over fat ties. She had found sad pictures of cheap looking suitcases lined up together – all the families' possessions, their whole life, reduced to this pitiful luggage, less luggage than on the average flight to Marbella these days she thinks. Another striking feature of the footage is how colourful the clothes were – in contrast to the rather drab outfits of the local population. There were all shades of blue, pink and orange cardigans and coats as well as the brightly coloured saris. How alien they must have looked!

"The Asians who came at that time were largely wealthy, successful and influential people who had run their own businesses and owned successful shops like the Bombay Stores." She explains to Priya who is half listening, half catching up on what Peter Andre has been doing. She will do more on her Mary Secole essay later.

"They were expelled virtually overnight by a man who had been trained by the British army! So much for his loyalty to Britain! Amin called the Asians blood suckers and said they dominated the best jobs. He claimed they were milking the economy."

"So why did they come here? To the UK I mean?" Priya's family never discuss what happened.

"They had British passports."

"And what sort of reception did they get?" Priya thinks she knows the answer to this.

"There was a lot of rage and anti-immigration feelings ran high. There were demonstrations as people feared for their jobs and the effect on housing and schools." She tells her. "I read that the meat porters in London, at Smithfield, marched on Westminster with placards saying "End immigration and start repatriation."

"Charming!" says Priya.

"But because they were good businessmen they persuaded bank managers to lend them money to set up businesses." Rita tells her. "That was how my grandfather raised the funds for his first corner shop on Evington Road." She said. (Whenever Mohal was avoiding his studies Jahi would remind him that he, Jahi, had worked in the corner shop before and after school and at weekends and still got a place at Sheffield to study dentistry! There was a picture in the study of Jahi's parents beaming proudly at his graduation ceremony.)

"Hello girls." Mr Payne, who runs the practice with his wife, strolls over. He has finished with patients for the day and welcomes a distraction before starting on the paperwork.

They chat about school and Priya's aspirations for a medical career- as well as history she is studying all the sciences. Rita has a question – could you fall backwards? Priya sighs at her friend's tenacity.

"Well it's unlikely but not impossible I suppose." Mr Payne says. "You tend to fall with your momentum. Most people on normal surfaces, if they fall they go forwards. That's why people break their wrists or arms. Think of a child who stumbles. When they realise they've fallen it's often because they can see the holes in their tights or the grazes on their knees. That's when small children really start wailing. Even what is called a 'sudden drop' – say a person's blood supply is cut off for a moment - will tend to lead to forward motion. People sometimes hurt their nose or their spectacles bruise their face." He is starting to look a little puzzled at Rita as he speaks.

"So the main reasons for falling backwards would be

because you were on slippy ground – ice or snow say - your feet literally go from under you then your weight carries you backwards. Or you might be struck or pushed from the front. That would do it." He finishes. "Can you tell me why we are discussing this?" he adds as Priya's mother appears.

* * *

Later that day, after she has been dropped at home by Priya's mother, Rita is in her room preparing her bag for the next school day. She wonders if Padma's obsession with altering and extending their house stems from her experiences in Highfields as a young child. From what Rita has read, the houses were of poor quality; the area had been used for various groups of immigrants, including those who were Irish and Jewish. So many families were crowded together! That was when Belgrave Road started to take off, Rita knew from things Jahi had said. The development of shops selling saris and religious paraphernalia, vegetables for the food the Asian families were used to, gradually these outlets had snaked their way along Belgrave Road until the whole area was like a street in Calcutta, an exciting place to shop, teeming with colour and vibrating with activity. It was a great centre for celebrations such as the Diwali festival which was now the biggest in Europe, amazing to think of it after those small beginnings. The newcomers crammed into Highfields could not have imagined how areas like Belgrave Road and other parts of the City would be transformed.

Rita looks at her timeline for Claire's disappearance based on what she has gleaned from the police and from the newspaper reports, trying to bear in mind the potential unreliability of the latter since their purpose was to attract readers. She has seen enough CSI know you need a timeline. Claire was born in September 1956, went to a local junior school and then to a girls grammar school in the centre of town when she was 11; she started working in a shoe shop on Saturdays when she was 15, which you could do in those days. For Claire to get a job she must have needed the money, Rita thinks, just like Jahi's family needed him to work in the family shop all those years ago. Rita thinks she is lucky. Her parents provide for her and her brothers, they have never needed to work and can concentrate on their studies (not that Mohal did of course, which was why her parents encouraged him to work at the library –"maybe some of that learning will rub off").

On 12 February 1972 Claire was seen to get a bus into town, just as she would if she was going to her job at the shop (it was a Saturday). But she never arrived. No one at the shop raised the alarm – the senior assistant thought she was ill or just not coming in for some reason. There seemed to be no evidence of what had become of her on that day. There was no CCTV in those days, either in the shop or on the streets. The police would have had nothing to go on. Her family did not get concerned when she didn't come back in the evening, which Rita finds odd, her parents would surely notice if she, Rita,was gone? Wasn't the school concerned? Or social services? The police weren't involved until the Monday but what did they do? And why did they find nothing again in 1990? All that time!

Rita thinks about her history essay. In 1972, she has found, Idi Amin was threatening the Indian community in Uganda with violence and effectively threw them out of the country. Leicester City Council had placed adverts to deter the expelled Asians from coming to the City. Why had they done that, she wonders. It must have reinforced the fears of those who marched against the influx, like those meat porters. Why would the authorities do that? How safe would those Indian families have felt when they did arrive? Were they resented? No wonder they settled where they had family and friends. You would want to be among people like yourself, people who accepted you, and have access to food and clothes that were familiar.

Was that part of Claire's problem (identify with the person and the context – Mr Thatcher again) Did she try to run away? Maybe she didn't feel safe? Or loved? It looked like she had come to harm in the woods by Bradgate Park – although nothing about what happened was certain. So if she went there, why? And why on that day, when she was due at work? Was there anyone she could have been meeting there? A boyfriend? Someone from school – another girl, perhaps, someone who was jealous of her, you saw that on Facebook all the time- or a teacher perhaps (there was that case recently where a girl went to France with her teacher) or someone from the shoe shop?

"Where is the truth?" Rita thinks.

Chapter

8

"I ground my faith upon God's word and not upon the Church"

Lady Jane Grey

5th November 1971

"Where's Claire?" Melanie was in the kitchen putting sausages in to the oven for the hot dogs they would eat later.

"Your Dad will be home soon and then we can light the fireworks."

"Hurrah" the twins were as excited as always on bonfire night, and ran upstairs to look out of their bedroom window to watch the flares rising into the sky. The Roberts family at number 6 had already got their fireworks underway and the boys could see their children, Susan and Michael, running round the garden with a sparkler each while their father struggled to light a Roman Candle. There was no bonfire in their garden. Just as well, Philip had said the year before, Norman Roberts would only set fire to the fence.

As he came into the house, having propped his bike against the wall by the back door, Philip brought with him the acrid smell of a thousand bonfires across the City.

"Oh, you're here." Melanie's tone was accusatory. "But still no Claire."

"Maybe there's a problem with the bus." Phil took his daughter's side. "It's only 6 o'clock,"

"Yes, exactly." Melanie, whose schedule was at risk of disruption, put her hands on her hips, her oven gloves dangling from her hip like a tail.

"6 o'clock!" she repeated as if the facts spoke for themselves

– "what can she be doing at this time?"

Philip went upstairs to get changed, the boys put on hats, gloves and coats and ran into the garden. "You'll catch cold." Melanie warned them but they took no notice, enervated by the excitement.

Claire entered via the back door just as Phil came downstairs, pulling on the blue sweater which Melanie had knitted for him a few years ago. "Hello, love." He got in before Melanie snapped "Where've you been?"

"Oh, I was just watching the start of the bonfire on the green." Claire said, "I saw it as I went past. I thought you wouldn't mind. I made sure I got back for six."

"Well it's gone six now." her mother observed pedantically. "And I was expecting you before now."

Claire knew better than to antagonise by adding a riposte; she turned on her heels and went to her bedroom to put down her satchel and change into trousers before emerging clad in her duffle coat and woolly hat and going to join her brothers outside.

* * *

While on the green by the shops earlier, watching the organisers light the large bonfire, Claire was aware the evening was especially cold. She had however been warmed by the proximity of Alex and their first kiss, made the more dramatic by the darkness interrupted frequently by loud bangs and flashes in the sky.

They had met in town for a milkshake – Alex having got permission to leave work early – and he had brought her back on his motor bike. While they were in the café, run by a local Italian family, and drinking with two straws from the same strawberry mixture out of an art deco glass, who should enter but her art teacher Mr Clarke! Claire had sensed her face going as pink as the drink. There was no time to hide. Robert Clarke stopped walking when he saw her, and adapted himself to the scene. The last girl he would have expected… but girls will be girls, he thought.

"Hello Claire" he said brightly, aiming not to sound censorious; although she did not know it, he needed Claire's goodwill as much as she needed his, given that the woman he was meeting was not his wife. Claire hoped he would not say anything to her parents, after all the next parents evening was not until January, plenty of time for him to forget. Mr Clarke spied Virginia at a table across the room; this is awkward he was thinking. Would Claire say anything about seeing him here?

As he carried two frothy coffees back to their table a few moments later he stole another glance at Claire, noticing for the first time what a very pretty girl she was. He had told himself that he was probably safe, the state of his marriage not being common knowledge. He need not have worried, he thought, the girl seemed transfixed by her companion – who was he? He looked a bit older than her although it was hard to tell these days the way boys grew their hair long, like those pop stars. Robert Clarke wondered how girls like Claire found this attractive; to his mind they looked more like girls than boys. Judging by the helmet on the seat next to the boy he had a motor bike. The teacher sensed that Mr and Mrs Watson were probably unaware that Claire was out with the young man. From the brief time they spent together as last year's parents evening he had got the impression they were not likely to greet the situation with anything but disdain and disapproval.

Claire released her straw to take a breath, peering surreptitiously at Mr Clarke. Lynn would want all the details! The woman his was with – presumably his wife but how could you tell –had black hair piled in an elaborate bun on her head and wore glasses so that she looked like a brainy scientist. They were holding hands under the table, she realised, something she had never seen her parents do.

Finishing their milkshake, and looking forward to seeing each other at the shop the next day, which was a Saturday, they made plans to go out together one afternoon in a couple of weeks' time. Claire would find an excuse to leave school early and Alex would take an afternoon off work.

Chapter

9

"Masters, I have offended the queen and her laws, and thereby am justly condemned to die"
                    Lady Jane Grey at her execution

19th October 2012

"This way." Rita, along with Priya and Bandhu, Rita's uncle, is being led by a petite, neat, fair-haired woman called Olga (according to the name badge on her purple tabard which she wears over black trousers). She has blue Crocs on her feet which squeak slightly with every step she takes on the vinyl floor of the nursing home corridor. They are in Thurmaston, where Bandhu has brought them in the afternoon. The walls of the corridor, painted pale green, are interspersed with paintings, the subject of matter of which is hard to discern as Rita glances at them.

* * *

A week earlier, Rita had stayed behind after the History class to talk to Mr Thatcher.

Rita had to wait while Mr Thatcher replaced his papers in their file. She gazed out of the second floor window of the arts block; from there she could see the setting sun reflecting golden in the windows of the new houses opposite – houses built on what used to be the school's outdoor football pitches. Now they had a state of the art gym instead. The newly planted trees, thin trunks lashed to stakes much bigger than the trees, giving the effect of small women dancing with tall men, were now the only signs of nature on the site; the houses were just starting to be occupied, and some were still not finished, their roofs covered in green material with a moss-like appearance, and none of the gardens had been planted as yet.

Papers safely stowed, Mr Thatcher stood up. "Now then what can I do for you, Rita?"

"I have an idea about my 1972 essay." she told him.

"Oh." Mr Thatcher was intrigued.

Rita explained that her aunt's husband works for the health authority (she is a bit vague on what exactly Bandhu does). They had spoken on the phone (The full story, which she did not trouble Mr Thatcher with, was that Padma had mentioned her essay to Jaina who had mentioned it to Bandhu who had had an idea).

"I was at a nursing home the other day." Bandhu had said. "We usually stop to chat to the residents. I came across a man who used to be a local councillor." He smiled to himself when he recalled the encounter.

"Some of them have great stories to tell," he said to Rita, glossing over those who didn't, "And this old boy – Richard Gregson – was on the City Council in 1972. From what he told me he still has a good memory for what happened then. Sadly, he's in a wheelchair now, but his mind's as sharp as a tack. I can take you to see him and you can get some first-hand information for your essay."

"Mmmn" Rita was intrigued but apprehensive. She had never been inside an old people's home, though she'd seen them on TV, and she found the idea daunting.

"If you're interested I'll take you to see him one afternoon. You just need to get permission from the school to take the time off."

"Great." She said, trying to sound enthusiastic, although she had to admit that getting an afternoon off from school made the proposition more attractive. "Thanks."

As she left Mr Thatcher, his permission willingly granted

("Good to see such enthusiasm," he had said," You can get some first-hand information.") Rita went to find Priya. It had occurred to Rita that Gregson sounded a familiar surname. She searched her head for the memory; maybe the iPad would help later, it might be in her notes.

"You have to come too!" she pleaded with Priya, "Don't let me have to go alone!"

* * *

"The pictures," Olga has stopped, noticing Rita's interest in them, "are part of an exhibition on the subject of memory. We thought it appropriate as many of our residents have dementia and other memory-related conditions."

Now that Rita and Priya pay closer attention to the paintings they can see that they are attempts to represent what it might be like to be looking for answers in a deteriorating mind. There is one, for instance, where shapes are hidden by a sort of cloud. There's another where there are pictures of people with bodies but no heads. The feeling of ideas slipping away is represented in a further picture with words tumbling like water out of a jug. This must be what it is like to only half remember things Rita thinks; you don't have to be old or ill to get that feeling, look how long it took her to remember why the name Gregson was familiar. At last, after going through her notes on Claire, she had realised that this was the name of Claire's next door neighbour, from number 8; could it be the same man, or maybe a relation? She plans to find out.

They come to a glass door which takes them to a sitting room carpeted in shades of orange and red, like the fallen leaves of the season outside. Rita has wondered what to expect. When she was younger, Jahi's parents had become too frail to look after themselves and had come to live with them, her brothers sharing a rather cramped bedroom to accommodate them. In fact, neither had lasted long, her grandfather succumbing to a heart problem and her grandmother dying in the Leicester Royal Infirmary after a cancer operation 6 months later.

Elderly men and ladies (mostly ladies, Rita notices) are scattered across the room; some are at small tables in groups, knitting or playing cards or dominoes. Rita observes how well dressed they all seem – quite formally attired compared to the casual dress most people wear in the street these days. No jeans or leggings here! Classical music is playing in the background and Rita can detect the distant smell of fresh bread baking. Rita wonders what the residents have to eat, and then realises she is surprised that the pleasant odour of food is all she can smell; one thing she had been dreading was some sort of disinfectant smell, or worse.

 Richard Gregson, it turns out, is sitting in an open glass-roofed area, like a conservatory, looking out into the distance at the darkening day. Bandhu introduces Rita, then he and Priya go off to talk to the other residents; Priya joins the 'knit and natter' group while Bandhu learns the rudiments of Bridge.

"So, young lady," Richard Gregson leans forward, peering at Rita over half rim glasses, his forehead a mass of wrinkles with a few brown spots interspersed among them, a bushy grey moustache covering his top lip. "You want to know what it was like in 1972, when Idi Amin announced he was expelling Asians from Uganda ?",

As she gets out her iPad, Rita explains about the essay she is writing and also tells Mr Gregson that her parents were among those who came to Leicester that year.

"Bandhu – my uncle - said you were a councillor at the time?"

"Yes, representing the south east ward." The elderly man's voice is hoarse, coming from the back of his throat and he looks out of the window as if recalling the past.

"Edward Heath was the Prime Minister at the time," he went on, "Like rabbits in the headlights the Government were," he added contemptuously. "The people who were expelled had British passports. Naturally they wanted to come here. We couldn't stop them. Enoch Powell had spoken of dire consequences of too much Commonwealth immigration in his famous speech in Birmingham in 1968, as you must know young lady," Rita nods, "We wanted to avoid that."

"South-east, where is that exactly? Does it include Elm Drive? That's where I live." Rita's thoughts about her essay are temporarily abandoned. She is getting excited about the possible connection with Claire.

"Really? Whereabouts? We used to live in Elm Drive. We moved to Houghton in 2005, but I haven't been back there for a good few years." Mr Gregson looks wistful.

"Were you at number 8? We're at number 10." Rita is certain this is the neighbour. Bandhu looks over from his card game to see that his niece and the man in the wheelchair are getting on very well, not suspecting that the subject of their conversation has strayed from the intended topic.

"Well I never. How did you know that?" An amused smile spreads across Richard Gregson's face, temporarily erasing some of the creases. Then a look of realisation crosses his face and he nods "So you're the family that moved in next to us, they were called Patel. Your mother must have been pregnant with you at the time?"

"Yes, that's right." Rita is excited now. "So you must have known the family who were there before us?" she asks carefully, how much does he remember she thinks, recalling the paintings on the corridor wall, but also remembering that Bandhu said Mr Gregson was as 'sharp as a tack', whatever that means.

"Oh, yes, sad business." A cloud has come across Richard Gregson's features. "I saw on the news that they think the body they found was Claire. I always thought something had happened."

"So you knew her?" Rita's suspicions are confirmed.

"We moved in at about the same time - the houses were new then - August 1955 it was." Rita notices that, like her grandfather was in the habit of doing, to tell his story Mr Gregson has gone back to the beginning. "Mrs Watson – Melanie - had her baby almost as soon as they moved in, in September. Funny that she was expecting when they moved in, just like your mother was with you."

(Rita nods at the coincidence, quietly making a mental note to check the dates on the certificates she has obtained. Surely Claire's parents were married in June 1955, which means…)

"Claire was a delightful little girl," Mr Gregson is in full flow now, gazing into the distance as if looking into the past. "She had fair curly hair as a toddler, like a halo. It was a while before they had any more children – me and Betty, that was my wife, couldn't have any, but we didn't mind. The boys came along, when Claire was about ten. What were they called now?"

"Thomas and Gerald." Rita is pleased to be able to supply the information about the twins she has seen only on the screen.

"Oh yes, we thought that was a bit funny – Tom and Gerry, you know? Don't know if they meant it to be funny or not." Richard Gregson chuckles at the memory.

"It looks like Claire was last seen in February 1972. When did you see her last do you think?" Rita decides to interrogate her witness while she can, thoughts of her essay forgotten for the moment.

"Well I told the police when they came to ask - when was that now? 1990? A long time after she disappeared. I gather the family wanted to trace her because Melanie was so ill by then. I told the police I always thought it wasn't right."

"What wasn't right?" (So someone had harboured suspicions, perhaps, Rita thinks).

"Well, Melanie, her mother, was adamant that Claire had run off with a boy. And she said if that was what she wanted to do – to live in sin as she put it - then that was up to Claire and she'd have no more to do with her." he pauses a second or two,

"I know folk hold strong beliefs, but it seemed harsh to us. Would it have hurt to contact the girl?"

"And you last saw her?" Rita brings the subject back to her question.

"Well, that's just it. On the day she caught the bus." Richard Gregson answers as if he has already told Rita this.

Rita looks puzzled.

"That Saturday morning." he expands. "The last day she was seen. I saw her. I'd been to get the paper from the paper shop. Ooh it was a really foggy day, I remember, you know, like we get sometimes, seems to last all day."

"You saw her get on the bus?" Rita is adding to her notes.

"Not exactly but she couldn't have been going anywhere else. I saw her in Beech Grove and I saw the bus go only a few minutes later. They used to be ten to and twenty past."

Rita looks confused.

"The 79 bus. Ten to the hour and twenty past. Funny what you remember."

Mr Gregson's recall of the bus timetable is clearly unaffected by his age.

"I don't think she was happy though." he adds after a pause.

"Do you mean on that day or generally?"

"Oh, generally, I mean. We noticed it about 6 months before she disappeared. In the previous summer. Of course you hear rows and such like in the warm weather because windows are open and folk are out doors. Me and Betty used to say we would not have rowed with our children like

Melanie quarrelled with Claire."

"Well, all teenagers row with their parents sometimes, don't they?" Rita tries, remembering the arguments she had heard between her father and Mohal over the latter's laziness.

"We felt it was more than the usual, to tell the truth, duck." Robert Gregson's accent is getting more local as he recalls the altercations he heard coming from the other side of the fence while he weeded his flower beds and mowed his immaculate lawn.

"She seemed a good girl to me" he reminisces with regret in his voice, "She looked after those boys when her parents were out, she dressed smartly, not like you see young girls on the streets today. She was not the kind to mess about with boys if you ask me. That's why I was so surprised to hear her mother say it to her one day, "You behave like a slut. You will come to a bad end. Don't get trapped like I did."

(A slut? Rita is inclined to agree with Mr Gregson's scepticism. Mentally she weighs up the pictures of an innocent-looking Claire in the scrapbook pictures with photos of girls from school she sees on Facebook most days- no comparison!)

* * *

When tea arrives and it is time to leave, Priya has learnt to cast on and do stocking stitch and Bandhu has enjoyed several hands of Bridge, skilfully guided through the bidding system by a sprightly resident of 90 ('I'm 90 years old, you know!')

"What did you make of the old folk?" Bandhu asks in the car, "They seem happy?"

"It's a caring place" says Priya.

"I think some of them have adapted to living there, others are still regretting things from the past." adds Rita, thinking of what Mr Gregson had to say about Claire as well as his role as City Councillor. She recalls another of Padma's famous quotes. "Life and death, joy and sorrow gain and loss; these dualities cannot be avoided, learn to accept what you cannot change."

Rita thinks maybe those ideas sustained the Asians who came to England in 1972. Accept what is and then you can make the best of it. She has gathered from Mr Gregson, who is ashamed to recall it now, that the City Council, finding there was no national plan or support to cope with the anticipated influx of Asian families from Uganda, had first of all placed adverts seeking to deter those who were expelled from coming to Leicester. "We thought we as a City would be overwhelmed, you see. That there wouldn't be enough housing, or jobs or school places," Mr Gregson had explained.

Rita has seen the adverts in an article from the Leicester Mercury. It seems to her to play to all the fears of immigrants that you heard from UKIP and others today. The adverts would surely have made it harder for the Asian families who did come to be accepted? When it became clear that families were coming in considerable numbers - about 25,000 came to Leicester - and with virtually nothing but the clothes they stood up in, the City Council had very little prepared and, instead, Richard Gregson said, it was the Asians already settled in Leicester who accepted the situation, stepped into the breach and set up informal welfare arrangements. These had turned into the Welfare Boards as some money eventually trickled out of the Government to help with what, but for the ability of the community to pull together, would have been a major crisis. Mr Gregson had admitted to Rita that it was fortunate that those who came were ambitious and determined. They took any job to get a foothold and were hard workers, he said, even monotonous factory jobs, although many of them were well educated and had run their own businesses in Uganda. By 1973, he had said, amazingly almost all the refugees had found somewhere to live and a means of supporting themselves.

The Asian community had to get to grips with politics and practicalities and rose to the challenge, Rita thinks. Maybe that was a wake-up call to take part in the political processes, which many local Asians now did in the City and in Westminster? Rita knows these are issues for her to discuss in her essay; the point of today was to get evidence from a voice around at the time, and she has done that for both her projects!

As Bandhu drives the girls home. Rita also remembers what Mr Gregson had to say about his neighbour's daughter, Claire Watson,

"You never saw her with any boys?" Rita had asked him.

"Just the once" Richard Gregson shifted a little in his wheelchair, as if physically uncomfortable as well as feeling the mental discomfort of the memory. "I was in Beech Grove one evening when a motor bike drew up and Claire hopped off. There was a young man in a helmet in charge of the bike. They didn't really say anything to each other. She just got off and waved to him as she went round the corner into Elm Drive."

"Do you know when that was?" Rita was leaning forward as if to catch every detail she can.

"Oh yes, I can tell you exactly" was the surprising reply.

(Really, old people's memories aren't that bad, Rita had thought.)

"It was the autumn before she disappeared, November 5th. I remember because fireworks were going off in people's gardens. I mentioned it to Melanie the next day. I hope I didn't get Claire into trouble…"

Chapter

10

"The crown is not my right and pleaseth me not. The Lady Mary is the rightful heir."

Attributed to Lady Jane Grey
on hearing of the death of
Edward VI and her
proposed accession.

9*th* October 1971

Although the October day was cold and temperatures down to 32 degrees Fahrenheit were forecast for the evening, Claire was standing on the deck of the Sealink ferry, looking across grey waves rising and falling as the ship shuddered through them towards the French coast. Like dancers in a passionate *paso doble* each wave seemed to want to dominate the one before it. Some of the water hit the side of the ferry with a sharp slap. The outline of other ships could be seen on either side of the ferry, too far away to be made out distinctly.

Claire was on deck because sitting below with the rest of her class made her feel queasy. Melanie, who had once been on the Isle of Wight ferry, had advised her to seek fresh air and keep looking at the horizon if she felt ill. The other reason she was there was her growing feeling that the others were laughing at her. Without Lynn for moral support – her parents could not pay for the outing and, unlike Claire, she did not have a Saturday job to meet the cost of the day trip - she felt keenly the girls giggling behind their hands. She had heard them mock her scarf - the one she'd tied round her head to stop the wind blowing her hair all over her face and making it worse than usual. She'd copied a picture she'd seen in one of Melanie's magazines of Princess Anne similarly attired. So she didn't think she looked odd. But if they wanted to laugh at her, so what? To comfort herself, she thought of Alex. They had spent some dinner times together on a Saturday and sometimes he would walk her back to her bus stop. They liked similar music and films. She could talk to him.

Claire had been apprehensive about coming on the trip but she told herself it would be good for her French ahead of the mock O Levels. Who knew, she might pick up some vocabulary or phrases. When she had mentioned her fears to Alex in their dinner break he had encouraged her – "You should go, you'll love it." he said. Never having been abroad, Claire was uncertain what awaited them. Would she understand what people were saying, would they understand her? When she listened to French on the cassette tape Mrs James sometimes brought into class, it sound incomprehensible. Like someone had scrambled the sounds she thought she ought to know and she didn't have the means to unscramble them. Ideally, she would like to go round with a group - tag along with the others, let the confident ones do the talking while she drank it all in - but as the others were finding her so amusing that might not be possible.

Helen and Gillian had been to France before. In fact, Helen said she'd been to Paris several times (her father was a travel agent) so this was just a jaunt to them, a bit of fun at half term. Claire could not imagine what it would be like to take going abroad for granted. Gillian and Helen had proffered blue passports at the departure desk, like the ones you saw in films, while Claire had got a yearly one from the post office which looked little more than a piece of card with her photo on it. This was something else the others found a source of amusement.

Later, in the market place at Boulogne, Claire was surprised to find herself feeling at home with the sights and general hubbub. The busy rows, the hectic choreography of the stall holders, bending over the fruit and vegetables like those glass birds that looked like they were drinking water, they were not very different from their counterparts in the teeming Leicester market where Claire went most Saturdays in her dinner hour to carry out commissions for Melanie. There she would patrol the stalls to find the best prices for the items her mother needed, noting also the quality, and had no qualms in stepping up to the appointed seller and explaining her requirements. With a flick of the wrist, while looking out for other customers (or someone pilfering from the stall) the seller would whisk the goods into a brown paper bag, twisting the ends and place the bag on top of the stall while they took the offered cash and gave any change. Claire had a shrewd idea of how much a pound of bananas, say, or carrots, or, in season, tomatoes, should cost. This was because she was required to account to Melanie for the balance she took home and to itemise the cost of what she had purchased. If Melanie thought she'd paid over the odds she would express her displeasure.

The French stalls were decked out with different goods compared to Leicester market, but that was not the only contrast. The overall sound of the voices was intangibly different- the barking of offers so common in Leicester, one seller wanting their voice heard above the others to attract attention- was missing. The theatrical gestures of the Midlands fruit and vegetable sellers, exaggerated arm and hand movements, were replaced with what Claire took to be Gallic shoulder shrugs, as if the sellers were indifferent whether you bought or not. There was food available to eat, which was not common in Leicester Market. The smell of waffles and warm croissants was reminiscent of the smell of doughnuts frying which she'd noticed when she went to the fair with Kevin and Mark in the summer. They had watched the pale dough floating into the oil like mini life rafts, gradually browning as if they were getting a tan. Then the vendor would push the doughnuts along a mini conveyor and toss them in sugar before delivering the finished product to mouths which were salivating. In the French market the pastries were laid out on trays, still warm from the oven, the aromas rising into the air and mingling with the smells of unfamiliar meats and cheeses as well as the odours from garlic and onions which were hanging in strings over the stalls like Christmas streamers.

The other girls had managed to summon up enough French to purchase chocolates for their parents and an improbably large pink teddy bear as well as having consumed ice creams and pains au chocolat, revelling in the novelty. Claire had only a few francs - she had swapped them for a pound note with Helen – and used them to get a French loaf to eat on the way back, having devoured the sandwiches Melanie had made for her as soon as the queasiness from the ferry wore off. She also bought a couple of chocolate frogs for Tom and Gerry who had teased her that the French only eat frogs legs, and a post card of the market for Alex to show him what it was like.

On the coach on the way home – cosily ensconced in a light, warm environment which was propelled through the dark streets comfortingly after the draughty buffeting of the ferry - Claire sat next to Isabel, one of the least worst girls in the gossip group. Claire felt she had not increased her French vocabulary or tried out her accent but she had somehow absorbed the atmosphere of France, or at least the bit they had seen. It seemed to have a sound and a movement which was subtly different from what you found once you docked in Kent. She thought Boulogne might be quite an exciting place to live - chic and sophisticated compared to her home town. She was looking forward to sharing her experiences with Alex when she next saw him.

* * *

On the Monday of half term, Claire took her brothers into the town centre so they could all visit the central library. She left them in the childrens' section looking at picture books while she went to peruse the adult shelves, looking for more in the Hornblower series, which she was avidly reading her way through at the moment. Horatio would have had no trouble with sea sickness on the ferry! A lot of her friends favoured Georgette Heyer or Catherine Cookson but Claire found those tales based on romance repetitive. She preferred Hornblower's adventures on the high seas. Even at a younger age she had enjoyed adventure books, such as the Biggles series. These were tales the twins would soon be able to enjoy. She was looking forward to discussing those books with them when they were older.

The library, on the corner of Bishop Street and Bowling Green Lane, inspired feelings of awe every time she walked in and almost made her want to whisper. It was in a grand municipal style, having been opened in 1905, with wide corridors and impressive staircases. Some of the original white busts remained to decorate corners of the various rooms. When they arrived, the library was busy with mothers and children and there were queues at the polished wooden counter to get books stamped; everything worked on cardboard tickets, which the librarians stamped as well as the books so they could keep track of the return date.

Having made her selection, Claire went to find the boys and together they had their books stamped out by a portly woman with dark hair and a smile when she saw the twins. After that they made their way along New Walk, where Claire knew the boys would be safe as it was for pedestrians only, no cars allowed, so they were free to run around as they wished, subject to not knocking anyone else over. They made their staggering way past the regency-style buildings with their plain white fronts and metal balcony railings twisted into intricate shapes, the boys dodging and hiding behind the trees which lined the path.

Gradually they progressed to the museum, where Claire knew the boys would enjoy looking at the stuffed animals, and dinosaur re-creations. The museum, like De Montfort Hall which they would go towards next, had been built in the classical style, with impressive white pillars at the entrance. They boys called it 'the White House'. She herself liked to look at the mummies kept there and wonder who they had been and what kind of life had they led? It was as well that the boys had run off some steam on their journey from the library as the curators did not take kindly to small boys running round the museum. They expected the exhibits to be treated with respect and Claire spent the next hour making sure her brothers stayed quiet and providing explanations for the various items on display as the boys' reading skills were not up to deciphering the labels.

Their mother had given them sandwiches to eat, so leaving the museum, and after a customary examination of the two black cannons standing outside it, they continued along New Walk, past more regency buildings which were created as houses and now mostly served as offices, to De Montfort Hall and from there across to Victoria Park where they sat in the band stand to protect themselves from the hazy drizzle which had started to fall. Claire had all their books in her bag and they were starting to get heavy. When the meal was done the boys ran about a bit on the grass- the rain had eased off but the grass was fairly damp.

Claire stared across the flat green park where the grass had been cut short to facilitate ball games. Various pitches were marked out and there were a few goal posts in place. Had they brought a ball, no doubt the twins would be practising penalties or scoring into the open goal mouth and congratulating each other. Claire though it amusing that the boys pretended to be World Cup players – Bobby and Jacky Charlton - even though they were too young to remember the England World Cup victory – that was the year they were born. Claire could recall the event, her father having acquired a small black and white television for the occasion.

As she turned she saw the tall figure of Alex coming into view as he walked across the car park to the grass. He had said he would try to get to Victoria Park in his dinner hour if he could. When he was a little nearer he raised his arm in a wave and she lifted her hand to wave back. They smiled at each other as he approached,

"Hello" they exchanged.

"You made it." Claire said.

"I haven't got long." he answered.

Alex sat on the bench where Claire was standing and she sat beside him, keeping an eye on her brothers.

Alex offered to share some of his food with her and Claire joined in sharing a packet of crisps. The drizzle had eased but the wind was cold. Claire dared not let the twins run for too long as she knew her mother would be angry if they got mud on their trousers. Alex set off back to the shoe shop when he had eaten his dinner, but not before Claire gave him the post card from Boulogne which she had remembered to put in her handbag.

Chapter

11

"Her vast acquirement of goodness was her fall"
William Hone 1825
(inscribed beneath a portrait of Lady Jane Grey).

5th November 2012

Sitting in the café in her duffel jacket and jeans waiting for Mohal, Rita can hear around her a cacophony of voices, accents and languages. On the table next to her is a group of young men from Eastern Europe talking loudly and animatedly. Because she does not understand the language the speech sounds very fast to Rita. It seems that one young man is telling the others a funny story as suddenly they all throw their heads back and laugh loudly. The group know one of the girls who is serving at the counter and they call to her with snatches of the story when she has a moment to listen.

When hailed by another youth, who has dark skin and dreadlocks in his hair, so maybe not from Eastern Europe Rita thinks, they all change to a very local sounding English, with the flat Leicester vowels perfectly reflected in their inflexion. Rita's parents speak Gujarati at home sometimes and used it a lot when Jahi's parents lived with them so she is accustomed to people switching languages easily. In their advancing years her grandparents seemed to lose a grip on the English they had learnt and to be more at home with the language of their youth. This fits with something Rita heard when she visited Mr Gregson in the nursing home. Olga, who showed them round, had told them that some of the residents were originally from Poland – they came during the Second World War, and now they were getting older they were reverting to communicating in Polish. Olga said it was useful to those residents to have Polish care workers at the home. Maybe her parents would go the same way, Rita wonders. Just as well then that she and her brothers can converse in the other tongue.

A woman on the table next to Rita is absent-mindedly banging a coin on the café table over and over. Is she anxious? angry? absent-minded? Stop thinking about other people Rita says to herself, opening her iPad to use the Wi-Fi in the café. She has emailed herself some notes about Claire and she wants to check some details and add to them before the meeting tomorrow.

The police woman had called at the house again. She said they were no further forward with what had happened to Claire. ("Sherlock Holmes would have solved it by now" Nayan said afterwards.) She told them that Claire's brothers were coming to Leicester; they had waited until the police said they could arrange a funeral. The Inspector gave Jahi details of the hotel where the brothers would be staying. He and Rita will be meeting up with Thomas and Gerald tomorrow, the day after the Diwali lights are switched on.

"Really, Rita." Padma had said, she was not keen on this plan. "I know why you want to go." Rita had assumed her innocent expression "You are still trying to solve the puzzle of that girl's death. Well you won't get to the bottom of it. Too much time has passed."

"I have to try", replied Rita, then, quoting one of Padma's favourite sayings, she added, "After all, truth cannot be suppressed and always is the ultimate victor."

Padma had sighed with exasperation and shaken her head. This is what she used to say to the children when they tried to lie to her about their misdoings.

"Have the police traced the conductor?" this is Rita's first note. Claire was last seen getting the bus into the town centre on Saturday 12th February. Rita had found out in her research that a bus conductor had come forward in 1990 to confirm she rode on his bus. He said he had told the police about it in 1972, when they made their first inquiries. Imran Khan was his name. Was he still alive today, she wonders? The reports, unusually for the press, had not included his age. Rita had tried googling him but there were too many people with that name to make progress. As was not uncommon with newspaper reports, they did manage to make it sound as if there was something suspicious about the bus conductor.

"Have the police spoken to Alex again?" this is her second note. Alex worked at the shoe shop and may have been the motor bike boy mentioned by Mr Gregson and Mr Clarke. He at least could be questioned, unlike the mysterious John of the postcard who could not be found. Is he really not involved in her disappearance in some way?

"Why Bradgate Park?" is the next note. Did it hold any special significance for Claire or her family? Did she know someone living out there? Perhaps the brothers can cast some light on that.

"Did she go straight to Bradgate Park the day she disappeared?" Rita has written. Did she meet someone in the town? Was it a planned or spur of the moment thing? It was unlikely anyone could answer those questions, they would remain issues for conjecture.

Mohal appears – he is on a reading week from uni. He is wearing a thick jumper and a patterned scarf – he looks quite the student - and he gets their tea from the girl at the counter; he also brings those wafer biscuits he knows Rita likes to share. The place is a Caffé Nero but you can still see traces of its previous incarnation as Italian café. 'Muzelli's' still appears in the glass of the side windows. The café overlooks Leicester market where many Asian stallholders are plying their wares - clothes such as jumpers and cardigans, and coats, and purses, bags, mostly made in China, plus all colours and designs of sari material, and items to celebrate Diwali.

"Where are we meeting Mum and Dad?" Mohal asks.

"By the Stores". Rita does not need to explain which shop, by family tradition they know the one to which they give this name, "They said they'd get a place by the barriers so Nayan gets a good view." Rita tells him, sipping at her tea and opening the wafer biscuits. "I remember I used to get so excited about Diwali, the lights, the crowd, the atmosphere."

"I think Nayan's getting a bit old to get excited now," says Mohal, "But he doesn't want to upset the parents by saying so." Brother and sister nod conspiratorially; they can see their mother especially is reluctant to let their youngest sibling grow up.

"Uni ok?" Rita changes the subject.

Mohal shrugs "It's ok. Lots of different people .You'll have to come and visit some time."

"Different how?"

"Same but different, really. Lots of different backgrounds. And many Chinese students. So much Mandarin being spoken around you, sometimes you think you're in Beijing!"

"The course is good?"

"Yeah, really enjoying that." Rita thinks it is clear Mohal is settling down. At least he's not talking about police oppression all the time.

"We'd better go before it gets too crowded." Rita says.

The pair move off and walk to join the surging mob, making its way to the best spots on Belgrave Road to see the drummers and dancers and the kaleidoscope of the procession as it makes its way along under the array of lights.

Rita calls her parents on her mobile phone as they proceed with the throng, to get better directions as to where to meet. "Hey" they exchange, Rita and her mother simultaneously ending the call between them as they see each other. All around are excited faces animated with anticipation, groups of young people in jackets and children on the shoulders of fathers, boys wearing hats with flaps to keep their ears warm, girls with their heads tucked into fur lined hoods, older groups, recalling the excitement of Diwali from their youth. The air is full of aromas as the herbs and spices of the street food (cumin, cardamom, turmeric etc.) blend in the air. Soon the noise of the music arrives and with it the dancers and drummers, and the processions, whirling colours – turquoise, maroon, gold, pink, glittering, shining, spinning, like a fair- ground ride. There are stalls along the road selling Indian sweets and drinks. The drums beat rhythmically, mesmerisingly, hypnotically. Rita finds herself smiling. You can't help being caught up in the excitement and the joy. There was good food to look forward to back at the house afterwards. Padma would have prepared excellent dishes for them all to share as part of the Diwali celebrations. Maybe her masala or biryani and coconut flavoured sweets, Rita thinks.

* * *

The next day, Rita and Jahi are standing in the reception of the Leicester Mercure Hotel, which had once been The Grand Hotel, a grandiose construction from a bygone age of opulence in red brick and stone which has been updated inside for the twenty first century traveller. This is where Claire's bothers are staying. Rita is gripping the scrapbook, which she has put inside a plastic bag to protect it. She wonders what Thomas and Gerald will be like in the flesh. What do they remember of Claire? Not a lot, she thinks, as they were much younger than her.

The lift doors open and the two rather portly, middle-aged men from the Skype screen step out in 3D. Each would be unremarkable on his own, but together - exact replicas to the untrained eye - they tend to attract attention and several people stare as they stroll across the hotel lobby in matching

Burberry jackets.

"Mr Patel" one of them says, offering a hand for a handshake which Rita's father politely reciprocates.

"And Miss Patel. So kind of you to come" The other one gives a sort of bow in Rita's direction.

"I'm Thomas," one says,

"And I'm Gerald" the other says.

The Australian accents seem more pronounced now they are together in person, or is it the contrast with the gentle hum of the local accent all around them in the hotel which makes it seem so striking?

"We thought we might." says Thomas.

"Take a cup of tea in the lounge." Gerald finishes.

"If you have time?" adds Thomas.

"Well," Jahi is not prepared for this. Padma is shopping so there is no hurry to return and the eagerness on Rita's face shows her vote is for staying.

"Yes, let's do that." he says. The four of them troop into the high ceilinged room beyond the half glass doors where the leather sofas are largely empty. Rita is unsure how you get tea in a place like this, but as if from nowhere a member of staff appears. Thomas and Gerald order Earl Grey, Rita and her father opt for mint tea.

No one seems to know what to say next. "So the police have no more information about what happened? But you can go ahead with the funeral? That's what the Inspector told me." Jahi breaks the ice.

Thomas nods.

"Do they have any theories about what happened to her?" Rita plunges in, but before either twin can reply the tea arrives.

As Thomas and Gerald pour from their shared pot – a rather complicated diffuser affair which it takes them a while to work out how to operate- they tell their story, finishing one another's sentences as they go.

They live in Canberra now and work for the Australian Government. Both are qualified accountants. They left the UK in 1995, after the sale of the house. They explain this move, saying they felt there was nothing to keep them here in the UK and that they wanted the challenge of another country. (Rita thinks there may be more to it than they are saying.) No mention is made at any point in their narrative about wives or girlfriends. (Rita speculates silently that they are probably gay.).

They had gone to the police in 1990, when their mother was ill and they were not able to trace Claire. Their mother, who had suffered early dementia, was in the late stages of pancreatic cancer and close to death by then. That was when they had given the police the DNA sample which had enabled identification when the remains were found by the archaeologists. Poor Claire, they say; all the time they thought she was in Scotland, she was lying in the ground.

"Scotland?" Rita is curious again, "That's because of the post card?" she recalls the Skype conversation with the twins.

Well, the twins say, pouring themselves more tea, they had sold the house after their father passed away. He'd been getting more and more confused with early Alzheimer's and they only just moved him to a nursing home when he died. Maybe it was the move, they say, or maybe he never got over their mother's death, even though they hardly spoke when she was alive and when they did it was to criticise each other. The twins are revisiting their childhood as they speak. It was when our mother fell ill with cancer, and the doctors said there was no hope, that we tried to contact Claire. Whatever had gone on, you see, we thought the two of them should have a chance to speak.

("What had gone on?" Rita thinks but allows the men to continue their flow.)

"So we made some inquiries,"

"Put ads in Scottish newspapers and eventually hired a

detective,"

(A private detective! Rita thinks, she must tell Nayan.)

"But he drew a blank. The trail was cold. That's when we asked the police if they could help. We never thought she'd be… well… that she'd be found like she has been…"

"We thought maybe they could ask all the police forces, maybe someone else was looking for her."

"Your parents didn't know where she was?" Jahi this time.

"Well, no, none of us did. All we had was the post card."

"When did the post card arrive?" Rita cannot help herself.

"The day she went – or the day we knew she'd gone - it was a Sunday. We were playing in the back garden. Dad came out, had we seen Claire? Did she go out earlier?"

"Well, no we hadn't. Mum was inside looking up phone numbers for the parents of her friends. She dialled everyone she could think of; no sign of Claire."

"It wasn't like her, you see. Second Sunday of the month, family service at St Andrew's, 11 o'clock. We always went."

"So in the end, we went without her. Mum and Dad in a foul mood. They spoke to several people at the Church, no luck. We both thought she'd be at the house when we got back, but she wasn't."

"Dinner and tea were especially bad that day, Mum was in a terrible mood."

Both men wince at the painful memory.

"Didn't your parents contact the police?" Rita says.

"Well apparently they did. We were only 6 at the time, of course, so we didn't know what was happening. When we went to the police in 1990 they said they thought there was a previous inquiry, but the records had been lost. Dad said he couldn't remember exactly what happened when they went to the police – with our mother dying it was a very fraught time for him. "

"On the Tuesday – or maybe the Wednesday - anyway, later that week, when we came back from school Mum said it was ok, Claire was in Scotland, and she showed us a postcard."

"Did you read it?" Rita is intrigued.

"Well, we didn't read much then and Claire's writing was very small. I doubt we could have made it out." Gerald.

"Later, much later, when we were about 10, we were in bed when we heard our parents arguing. Dad had said something about contacting Claire and Mum said something like "She's not crossing my threshold. She's made her bed and she can lie on it. I told you before, no daughter of mine is going to live in sin and then walk into my house." Thomas.

"Of course, we didn't know what living in sin meant then…" says Gerald.

It was clear from the way the men recounted this row that as small boys it had made a strong impression. Rita pictures them cowering under their bed covers while the row shook the house.

"…and nowadays it seems ridiculous, but Mum believed in Church and all that, even though she only went occasionally, Christmas and Easter and the family services. She didn't think it was right to live with someone without being married."

(The brothers are looking at each other with raised eyebrows. Rita thinks "They never told their mother they were gay, either – if they are gay, of course.")

"So your parents weren't exactly hoping that Claire would make contact?" Rita asks, "They weren't jumping every time the phone rang in case it was her?"

"Well, no." Thomas admits.

"But that was probably because of what the postcard said." adds Gerald.

"We know, or think we know, what the post card said because Dad told us." The brothers continue. "When we got the police involved in 1990 he said" don't do that, she doesn't want to be found, that's what the post card said." Thomas explains.

"It was a card from Scotland?" Rita clarifies.

"Yes, It was a picture of Edinburgh Castle – we remember that- and it must have had an Edinburgh post mark as Mum and Dad showed it to the police in 1972 and we think that's when they stopped investigating."

"Dad told us she'd written, I've gone to Scotland to live with John. Don't try to find me."

"Who was John?" Rita searches her memory but does not recall any mention of John by the police, or in the newspaper reports.

"We didn't know. Mum and Dad didn't know. No one seemed to know – not our aunt or anyone at the shop. But no one seemed to try to find her after that. She'd obviously run away of her own accord."

"And in 1990, when you asked the police to help trace her? Was John found then?"

The twins shake their heads. Claire's whereabouts had remained a mystery. The post card could not be found and there was no record of the 1972 inquiry. In 1990 the police had traced the manager from the shoe shop, who was still living in Leicester, well in a village outside, in Broughton Astley. Ian Sharp was his name. He had worked for various shoe companies over the years – the companies kept going into liquidation in the light of competition from abroad. He had told them he still recalled Claire and the day she did not turn up which was so uncharacteristic. He was as puzzled as everyone else about why she had not gone to work or where she had gone to; he did not know of any John and had never heard Claire mention that name.

He apparently told the police that Claire seemed sweet on another sales assistant, called Alex Podolski. The brothers said that the police inspector looking into what had happened to Claire now had looked at the 1990 records and was hoping to contact Alex. He had married apparently and he, too, had moved around in the Leicester area so it was possible he had seen the publicity around the discovery of the remains. In 1990 Alex had said he went to the shop as usual that Saturday. He was going to a folk concert in De Montfort Hall that evening with his mother, so he had gone in on the bus rather than on his motor bike. According to his statement in 1990 he was shocked by Claire's non-appearance. It sounded as though they had been keen on each other. Alex told the police he had got up the courage to go to Claire's house, but was so intimidated by the thought of her parents that he had not had the nerve to knock on the door. He also went to Claire's school and spoke to her friends; that was when he realised she had vanished.

"Did the police have statements from anyone else do you know?" Rita is leaning in, trying to recall as much as possible so that she can make notes later on their iPad. Jahi is crossing his legs, trying to signal to Rita not to be so intrusive.

"The bus conductor for example?" (Rita, ignoring her father, is recalling the questions she wrote down the day before.)

"Some teachers from her school, I think they said." The twins search their memories. Her form teacher and an art teacher was what they came up with. One of them had seen Claire with a boy who had a motor bike helmet; this was probably Alex from the shoe shop (the same boy Mr Gregson had seen her with, Rita thinks). The form teacher had died in the intervening years; Mr Clarke the art teacher was nearly 80, the brothers said the police had reported, but he remembered Claire. The brothers give a joint sigh.

"How did she die, exactly?" Rita wants to check what the brothers know against what she has read and heard.

"Hard to tell after all this time. All they've got is the fracture to the back of the skull. The only other mark is the wrist fracture which she did when she fell on ice years before." Thomas tells her.

"Now, let's have a look at Claire's scrapbook?" Gerald asks.

The brothers, finally satiated with Earl Grey tea, both make a gesture like rubbing their hands and Rita produces the plastic bag with its contents.

"I had another look at the postcards," she tells them "but there's not one of Edinburgh Castle." ('Why would it be here anyway?' she thinks, 'if this is Claire's collection.')

"Oh look!" the twins are delighted "This was Claire's." They flick through the scrap book together. "There's her tiny writing." They point to the small blue script on some of the pages, indicating the year of some of the photographs. "And this would have been done by Mum." They point to the larger, italicised handwriting, "calligraphy was one of the things she studied at night school."

"There's our parents on a day trip to the sea." They are looking at the first photographs, and there's us, and there's Claire." The faces of the men soften as they look at their lost sister.

"It is lovely to see these old photos. There we are on holiday – look!"

"What were your parents like?" Rita ventures to ask, keen for any clues as to what went on all that time ago and to check the picture Mr Gregson had painted for her. The men look at one another. Thomas starts – this seems to be an agreed pattern.

Their father, it turned out, had spent a lot of time in his shed ("I remember the shed" says Jahi). He collected lots of things, old record players and pieces of string. He was affected by his wartime childhood and could not bear to let things go. Weekdays the boys were at school. Their mother dropped them off and picked them up and did odd jobs in between. She'd done make up demonstrations, sold things in the evening on the phone (we had to be quiet then as the phone was in the hall), helped with traffic censuses – sitting for hours in laybys counting cars - and delivered flowers for a local florist. None of the jobs lasted long. She wanted to 'improve herself' she used to say, which is why she went to night school. It was as if she had married too young or settled for the wrong man they thought now. Neither of them was happy it seems but couples stuck together in those days, the brothers say. (Rita remembers the dates on the marriage and birth certificate for Claire; Melanie being pregnant when they married may not have been an ideal start she thinks.)

"And no one tried to get in touch with Claire?" Rita tries one more time.

"Oh no. Well how would they have? And even if they could, our mother was very angry with her for running off. She said she'd let the family down. I remember her being particularly short with Aunty Elaine – mother's sister - when she raised the subject once. Mother would say even if she got in touch I wouldn't speak to her." Gerald speaks and Thomas nods in agreement.

With details of the funeral – which will be at the crematorium - Rita and her father leave the hotel twenty minutes later, leaving behind the two brothers still reminiscing and recalling events, memories prompted by the pictures. As she travels home with her father Rita reflects what a sad life Claire seemed to lead – they sounded a very unhappy family. Was that a reason for the brothers leaving the country – why they wanted a fresh start? Or was there more to it? Were they afraid about what might have happened to their sister? What was that saying she had heard Padma recite? She tries to recall, oh yes, "When the family is ruined, the timeless laws of family duly perish, and when duty is lost, chaos overwhelms the family."

Chapter

12

"That little week of splendour, forced and feared, so soon laid down, cost thee most bitter wages."
Martin Farquar Tupper 1860 on Lady Jane Grey

9th September 1971

On Claire's birthday, she got up at 6.30 as usual. It was a weekday so she dressed quickly for school and ate her toast, which she made under the grill, before leaving to catch her bus. The school she went to was 3 miles away, just far enough to get a free bus pass which was lucky said Phil "Cos we'd never afford the fares otherwise."

Her father would cycle every day to the textile factory in Wigston where he worked, supervising production of knitted garments. He took his bike come rain or shine, fastening clips to his trousers to stop them catching on the pedals. Her mother would drive the boys to their junior school, then go to whatever job she was doing at the moment, and collect them at 4. Claire rarely got a lift home. When she did it would be with friends, as today. Lynn and Marie were coming back for their tea in honour of her birthday.

Because it was her birthday, Claire found it hard to concentrate on her lessons. She was in the Upper Fifth form – the O-level year and had timetabled sessions all day Geography and History, then break time, double Biology, then dinner time, English. French and Maths to end the day. Most lessons were in the class room, the girls moving only to attend lessons in laboratories, the music, sewing or art rooms. This added to the staleness in the air in the room and general feeling of ennui. A bell indicated the breaks between lessons when a teacher would leave and another one arrive. At the start of each day most girls were required to file into the hall for a reading and some prayers followed by a hymn. The Catholic girls could opt out, if their parents wrote a letter, and spend the time in a room together reading their Bibles. The head usually took the opportunity of Assembly to upbraid the school for some indiscretion committed by a few individuals or about a complaint from the public. Today was no exception. Girls had been seen eating in the street in their uniforms. Anyone identified for this crime would receive a letter home. Two pupils then struck up a resounding march in duet on the piano and everyone left for the classes to start.

Claire had a desk near the door to the class room. They were arranged alphabetically and being a 'W', hers was the last but one desk, the end desk being occupied by Christina Zielinski. It meant that Claire was next to the radiator which was a blessing on cold days in the winter term. As it was September, the heating was not on yet; it would not be switched on until after half term.

The pupils stood up when a teacher entered the room, exchanging ritual greetings in the language in question with the German, Latin and French teachers. The dark skirts, white shirts and dark ties which they all wore, with a cardigan for warmth and sling purse for their dinner money, lent a military air to proceedings when they all stood to attention. Skirts had to be on the knee, a difficult rule to observe for girls who were growing or girls anxious to show off their assets. The rule was policed by Mr Frobisher who was not above getting out a ruler to check the length of a questionable skirt. Pupils in the first and second forms wore long white socks. From the third form (for historical reasons called the Upper Fourth) it was permissible to wear neutral coloured tights. The tights snagged frequently on the old wooden desks so it was a running battle to prevent them laddering to the extent that they disintegrated before the end of the day's lessons. Some girls delighted in the damage and would encourage ladders to form. Others, like Claire, had become adept at applying clear nail varnish to the first sign of a hole or ladder, thereby postponing the destruction. New tights were an expense her parents would not welcome and she did not want to spend too much of her hard earned money on something needed for school.

The French teacher was a younger one (Mrs James) whom they all liked. She brought a more relaxed air to the room and sometimes even sat on the teacher's desk – better not let the Head see that! Claire enjoyed her lessons the most. They were talking about the forthcoming day trip to Boulogne. Dinner had been quiche and salad with coleslaw (using up old veg, Lynn said) followed by a jam tart called 'Manchester grid' and thin custard; the smell of it lingered in the corridors in the afternoon. Claire would be glad when she was in the sixth form next year and could bring sandwiches, both because it meant it would save her parents money and because she would not have to eat things she did not like. All plates had to be emptied, which led to girls resorting to extreme measures - putting food in their pockets, scooping it onto another plate when no teacher was looking and so forth; the queue for the sick-room was especially long when liver was on the menu as was the propensity to faint in the dinner queue. No one was allowed out of Claire's school at lunch time. Some girls (the keen ones) would get a ball and play on the netball courts, others would walk around the building in an effort to keep warm. No one was allowed inside unless it was raining and they had the permission of the teacher who was supervising. On this day – her birthday – Claire was privileged to be carried along with the group in her year which dominated the bench by the Biology pond. The day was warm, the September sun still relatively high in the sky, and they spent the time imitating the groups they had seen on Top of the Pops the previous week.

When Melanie collected them in the Morris Traveller, Claire sat in the front, her friends in the back and the twins in the boot of the Morris Traveller, their legs intertwined, waving to the other cars from the back doors. The car nosed its way through the traffic like a pig searching out food, its deep engine noise throbbing in contrast to the more modern vehicles around it ("sounds like a Lancaster bomber." Phil often said.)

When they got into the house, Mum had laid the table in the front room, the room which looked out over the street and from which you could see the houses on the opposite side of the street. She'd used the "best" green table cloth (from her great aunt, when she died) and "best" tea service (from another dead auntie). There were ham and tomato cobs (that's what her mother called crusty rolls) and cheese and cucumber sandwiches, with a red jelly and homemade chocolate cake to follow. Mum let them play Claire's David Cassidy record on the record player. For once, the boys were not in the way. Mum made them play in the back room where they could be heard wrestling each other and running around. That room had the French windows, as her mother called them, leading in to garden, where Claire's father spasmodically tended a vegetable patch yielding (some years) onions and potatoes and her mother claimed to be trying to nurture roses and strawberries. Claire rarely went in to the garden these days. She found its wilderness embarrassing in contrast to the well-tended beds and trimmed lawns of Mr Gregson next door but the twins loved its overgrown foliage, giving them opportunities to hide, even if it also took them longer to find their ball because of it. Quite often their ball ended up in next door's garden and the twins would troop round to seek its return.

When she opened her presents, Claire found that Marie had given her a lipstick, Lynn a pen, and her parents a blue jumper. The present she liked best was the medallion from her Aunt Elaine, Mum's sister. It was copper in colour, shiny metal, with a galloping horse etched into it.

Mum drove her friends home while Philip did the washing up – the smell of his cigarette wafting through the house – and Claire put the boys to bed, first showing them her presents. Then she carried her new treasures to her room, the small one at the front of the house, next to her parents' room. Claire quickly took off her uniform, hanging her clothes on the back of the chair ready for the next day. She pulled a soft blue bri-nylon nightie over her head and wrestled her way under the covers on her bed. Quickly, before her mother returned, she took out the jewellery box from under her bed and looked at the card which she had been given on Saturday. Under the words happy birthday, Alex had written 'with love'.

Chapter

13

"For when I am in the presence either of father or mother, whether I speak, keep silence, sit, stand or go, eat, drink, be merry or sad, be sewing, playing, dancing, or doing anything else, I must do it as it were in such weight, measure and number, even so perfectly as God made the world; or else I am so sharply taunted, so cruelly threatened, yea presently sometimes with pinches, nips and bobs and other ways (which I will not name for the honour I bear them) ... that I think myself in hell."

Lady Jane Grey to the Scholar Roger Ascham

14ʰ December 2012

"How was the funeral?" Rita and Priya are walking together to the newsagents near the school. It is 11 am and they have no lessons to attend for a couple of hours. They are not the only pupils from their school in the street. Ahead are a couple of girls from the year below, distinctive by the hajibs they artfully combine with their school clothes. Rita has also seen Nayan in the distance (doesn't he have maths this morning?) but the siblings long ago agreed that what happens in school stays in school, none would report back to their parents what they saw or heard. The boys from school mostly wandered out nonchalantly around 11 o'clock to get chips – that was when the chip shop opened. Many would consume a school dinner as well, or spend the lunch hour cramming more calories in to their mouths – crisps, rolls, chocolate – you had to wonder where boys put it all thinks Rita, probably into all that growing, certainly Nayan must start to shoot up soon, he is getting left behind by his class mates. The numbers of pupils in the street is becoming resented by some residents, Rita knows; there have been meetings at the school and talks about 'school pastors' to defuse situations where excitement spills into aggression or potential criminal activity. She keeps this information from her parents, who would only worry and step up the protection they afford her even more. As it is, she is required by them to make sure she only goes out with Priya or another trusted female friend and her parents or Priya's make sure they are picked up from any late night or out of school activity.

Like others in their year, Rita and Priya do not wear uniform. The uniform for the rest of the school is a combination of grey trousers and blue sweat shirts. Rita and Priya now favour trousers or leggings and tops from Top Shop or Miss Selfridge. They wear boots on their feet most of the year, keeping their heels only for the warmest weather. Now they are in the sixth form they have 5 lessons most days, the lower school were supposed to have 8, all of 35 minutes duration. The experiment with pupils deciding whether they wanted to go to lessons had ended a few years ago and they were now required to attend, although no register is taken so no one actually knows where you were. The changeover between lessons led to a melee of pupils strolling to their next class room in which it was possible to disappear out of the gates without being noticed. Some schools had started using CCTV, Jahi had said the other day, and others had USA style security to check pupils for knives or other weapons. ("I don't know what the country is coming to." was Padma's reaction.)

Rita and Priya have already discussed the X Factor final on their accustomed walk to the newsagents where they found the staff were friendly and sandwiches and snacks could be purchased, including fruit and fruit drinks which the girls liked to have for the sake of their figures. "All boys." Priya had said "Yeh, all men, like the Bake Off final" Rita had added. Then the conversation had turned to the recently announced royal pregnancy. "I hope she has a girl." They had agreed.

"Weird, as you might imagine." Rita answers her friend's question about Claire's funeral.

"At least she had some family there," replies Priya, "Imagine what it will be like when they bury Richard III."

"When they've decided where to bury him of course," Rita adds.

"Yes, well the Church or Cathedral or whatever will be full of those Richard fanatics, the ones who got the money together and pursued the idea until they dug up the car park. There won't be any family."

"Well, duh, of course not…Not unless the Queen comes" Rita adds thoughtfully, "Are they related?"

"Dunno. S'pose they must be. But what I mean is, no one who knew him."

"Well they would be pretty old by now. And I agree the Richard III Society looks a bit crazy, but look at the care they took when they thought they'd found him; that woman insisted they put a flag over the box they put him in. She did try to treat him with the dignity a King might expect."

"Do you think he'll stay in Leicester?"

"Who knows? If we apply RSVP he'd probably vote for York, according to what people say. But then he wouldn't have voted to lose the battle and die so horribly would he? I read that they will try to put together a service that reflects the practices of his time. This was before Henry VIII and his split from the Pope."

"Oh yeah – can't exactly give him a Humanist funeral can they! So what kind of service was it for Claire?"

Rita starts to recount her afternoon at the crematorium. Jahi had cancelled some patients so he could come with her ("You are getting obsessed like your daughter." Padma said "Claire's been dead for years and we didn't know her.")

* * *

As Rita and Jahi waited outside the chapel at the crematorium they saw a group of mourners leaving. They were probably the group they had spotted earlier as they were parking; the coffin which went inside after them had DAD on its side in blue and white flowers. The group was mainly overweight women squeezed into black dresses which in Rita's opinion were far too revealing of flesh - especially cleavage - for a funeral and young men with tattoos on their necks and at least one earring each. Rita thinks it likely that when they had smoked the cigarettes they were all desperate to light as soon as they left the chapel they would be moving on to a pub.

"It is ok for us to go in?" Rita checks with Jahi again.

"Oh yes, no one minds. It will probably be a few words and then the coffin goes behind a curtain." her father explains, having attended similar ceremonies for colleagues from the dental practice.

Thomas and Gerald arrive at the same time as a car carrying a white coffin on which is tastefully placed a pink wreath. Rita thinks the remains must be rattling around inside a coffin of normal size but tries to dismiss the image. The brothers clearly want to do what is right by their sister. They are formally dressed in dark suits and their hair looks more grey today. As Rita looks from them to her father she thinks it strange how close in age they all are, the brothers were born only a year before Jahi, and yet with their heavier build and hair colouring the twins look much older, Jahi retaining an upright and distinguished look while the twins look bowed down by life, or maybe it is just the cares of this difficult day.

"Thanks for coming." Thomas acknowledges them as the brothers file into the chapel. Rita realises the couple who were standing near them are coming in too – she thought they belonged to the previous funeral - the man has grey hair and is wearing a suit, the woman's hair is white and she wears a fur jacket over her black dress; she looks a lot older than her companion and he is supporting her as they walk along. The couple are followed by the blond police woman. So 7 mourners in all.

Rita finds the sparse ceremony, conducted by a woman in a long black coat, strangely moving. The woman incants various phrases, some of which strike a chord with Rita -

"We brought nothing into the world, and we take nothing out."

"The Lord gave, and the Lord has taken away; blessed be the name of the Lord."

"Blessed are those who mourn for they will be comforted."

"In sure and certain hope of the resurrection and eternal life."

Rita is not sure whether Claire entertained any hope, but the brothers said their mother "believed in all that religious stuff" and would have wanted a Christian ceremony for Claire. The female Minister speaks of Claire's life, tragically cut short; how she never got to fulfil her promise; she skirts around the circumstances in which the remains were found, saying only, "her family missed her" (well some of them did thinks Rita) and the mystery of her absence was now solved so that they were able to lay her to rest. Then comes the finality of the curtains closing, knowing the coffin is bound for the flames.

Rita thinks, wherever Claire was going next, she has long since gone. She finds herself saying in her head -

"From untruth lead us to Truth. From darkness lead us to Light. From death lead us to Immortality. Peace, Peace, Peace. Be at Peace Claire."

When the funeral is done, Rita and Jahi stand around for a bit, together with the brothers and the couple, who when names are exchanged turn out to be Alex Podolski, Claire's boyfriend by some accounts, and his mother. (So the police have traced him again, Rita notes.)

"That's that." says Thomas, with a sigh.

"I guess we'll never know what happened to her." says Gerald resignedly.

"Bradgate Park is the key." pipes up Rita. "Did you ever go there?"

Jahi shuffles with discomfort, surely he and Rita have had this conversation? Don't bother everyone with your questions!

She had addressed the question to the brothers and is surprised when both Thomas and Alex speak together -

"Yes."

"Oh?" Rita turns to Alex, "Do you mean you went with Claire?"

"That's right." Alex speaks slowly, clearing his throat nervously, "It was all such a long time ago but I can see her now, climbing on to the back of my old Honda motor bike. We both liked the countryside here, the space, the chance to get away." He glances cautiously at his mother, even at his age - what? 60 something years old? - he was remains anxious not to upset her feelings Rita observes.

"We came when we first started, I don't know, getting to know each other I suppose. Around November time. Then we met here again after Christmas - Claire's last Christmas as it turned out. We just looked around and talked, nothing else." he adds defensively.

"And you didn't plan to run away together? Or to meet her to day she disappeared?" Rita asks two questions at the same time and Jahi gives his daughter a dig in the ribs – she has gone too far!

"Oh no. The police asked me that. We did talk about going together to Paris - the way you do when you are young, I mean and nothing serious. That day, though, we had no agreement to meet. I was expecting her at work – at the shoe shop. When she didn't turn up I was concerned, of course. I tried to get up the courage to speak to your parents" He nodded to Thomas and Gerald, "But I was too afraid, or too young, or something. I wish I had now…"

"It wouldn't have made any difference." Gerald is reassuring.

"But she might have been found sooner. If everyone understood she had not gone away deliberately."

"Well…" Thomas begins to examine the situation, Rita can see Jahi getting restive.

"And you came to the Park as well?" she intervenes to ask the brothers.

"Yes we did sometimes go on family trips, when we were very young, but they stopped after Claire disappeared." Gerald answers.

"Yes, we never went to Bradgate after that." Thomas concludes.

* * *

A fortnight later and Rita is in the kitchen at home.

"So who's in the frame?" Mohal, back from Uni for the Christmas break, ("I don't know why we pay for that accommodation!" Jahi says) is taking a casual interest in the papers Rita has strewn over the table. Print-outs from back copies of the Mercury, her timeline, copies of some of the pictures from the scrapbook and various names written on Post-It notes are among the documents she is assembling.

"I've got various ideas." Rita replies.

"Hmmn." Mohal is not really listening, he is flicking through a Men's Health magazine, wondering if he should go to the gym at Uni after Christmas; they have the latest equipment and a large swimming pool, all on campus.

"So you're sure she was murdered? It wasn't an accident?" This from Nayan who sits at the table, his head resting on his hands.

"Well an accident is just about possible I suppose but it seems unlikely. From what the osteopath told me it's more likely she was hit or pushed." Rita pauses, "And I just think the brothers must have sensed something was not right."

"Bit harsh." says Mohal "What do you mean?"

"Well why the move to Australia? It's a long way. It's as if they were running away from something. Trying to make a fresh start".

"So, who's in the frame? This is like 'Law and Order' innit?" Nayan likes to watch crime programmes, especially when there are gory details of how the person died. He is now on the tiled kitchen floor, practising hand stands, trying to do it with one hand in emulation of Louis Smith, the Olympic medal winner, who Nayan has glimpsed on Strictly Come Dancing which his mother and sister watch.

"There are a few possibilities." Rita is finding this discussion helpful in clarifying her thoughts. Strange how ideas feel like a thick fog swirling in your mind and how the fog clears so you can see your way when you start to say them out loud.

"Remember I told you about the post card from Scotland?"

"The one her brothers described?" Mohal shows he is still half listening at least.

"But it wasn't in the scrapbook." Nayan's tone is strained as he is upside down as he speaks.

"Well if Claire didn't send it because she was dead, someone else did."

"Aah" says Nayan, turning upright again and thinking he has found a flaw in the argument. "How do you know Claire didn't go to Scotland and then come back?"

"I don't know for sure," Rita admits, "But does it sound likely? Why say you're running away and then come back?"

"Because she changed her mind?" Mohal offers not unreasonably.

"Yes, but then she'd go home, surely? Why go to Bradgate Park?"

"Well, why did she go to Bradgate then ?" Nayan challenges his sister.

"That's a good question." agrees Rita, putting the tips of her fingers together as she has seen David Suchet do as Poirot.

"I asked people at the funeral whether they had been to the Park. Alex Podolski was there – the guy from the shoe shop – and it turns out he did go there with Claire a couple of times. But he denied arranging to meet her that day, the day she left the house and never came back. So was he lying? Or did she go there to meet someone else?"

* * *

"How is CSI going?" says Priya sarcastically on Facetime later that day. Rita is sitting at her desk in her bedroom, looking out into the late afternoon darkness, the street lamp casting an orange glow on the road surface which is glistening as a frost forms - the gritting lorries have been out on the main roads, ice is expected by morning. Priya by contrast is finding it stiflingly hot at her uncle's house in Mumbai where her family are staying for the holidays. She has escaped a family discussion to talk to her friend from the guest room but the walls are thin and the family's conversation penetrates through.

"Are you going to tell me who you suspect or not?" (It is 10 o'clock in the evening with Priya and 5 o'clock in the afternoon in Leicester).

"Well," says Rita, looking up her notes, "John is the obvious suspect. The one she mentioned in the post card."

"The one from Edinburgh?"

"Yes, according Thomas and Gerald, the post card, which arrived a few days after she disappeared, said she had run away with John."

"Well then..." Priya interjects.

"Yes, except that the twins do not remember anyone called John, and while they may have been too young to know what Claire was up to, when the police looked into it all in 1990 they did not identify a John either. So he may exist or he may be a red herring."

Priya sighs. "Random. This is well hard. So she made him up?"

"I think that's likely. Sources and voices remember. Who said there was a John – Claire. Why would she say that? Either because it's the truth - but if so no one has found him - or to put her parents off the scent? Don't you think if he existed there would have been some evidence?"

"John was someone else?" Priya again.

"Or nobody." Rita is proud of this train of thought. "Just because she said she was running away with someone doesn't mean she was."

"Yes." says Priya not sounding convinced, "I guess that's an option. But did she have any money? How would she have managed on her own?"

"I agree that's a flaw" concedes Rita "It's not the likeliest scenario but it can't be ruled out."

She looks again at her notes on the iPad.

"The main point is – whether she went away or not, whether she went alone or with someone - the only reason you can think of for her being in Bradgate Park would be to meet someone, you wouldn't go there on your own, especially in winter and especially when she should have been going to her job. That's not to say the person she met, or was due to meet , caused her death, it's possible she went there and came across a nasty stranger, you hear about cases like that."

"So if not John, who else? Who was she planning to meet? And if she didn't turn up because of this 'stranger danger' theory, why did not they raise the alarm?" Priya is trying to follow this while she can also hear that her family's conversation in another part of the house is becoming animated - something about the best way to prepare chickpeas?

"There's the one who admits to being a sort of boyfriend, Alex."

"The one from the shoe shop? Who you met at the funeral? Is it suspicious that he came to that? Guilty conscience?" Priya asks.

"Hardly likely! He came with his mother!" Rita ripostes.

"Was she keen on him? Claire I mean?" Priya is curious.

"It's hard to know how close they were. Alex said they were 'getting to know each other' but who knows what that means. They tried to keep it a secret from her parents – Alex says he was scared of them - but there were some witnesses." Rita tells her.

"Witnesses?" Priya wonders what her friend means.

"Well, Mr Gregson - the neighbour I went to see that day we went to Oak Trees - told me he saw her with a boy on a motor bike and that tallies with Mr Clarke's statement to the police in 1990." Rita starts to sound very organised in her research.

"Mr Clarke? Who's he again?" Without the benefit of Rita's notes, Priya is finding this difficult to follow.

"That's the art teacher. We'll come to him soon. According to the newspaper report, Mr Clarke said he saw Claire in Muzelli's – the Italian café that used to be near the market, it's a Caffé Nero now - you know where I mean?"

Priya nods, "Mmmn. I think I know..."

"According to the newspaper report, Mr Clarke said he went into Muzelli's on bonfire night – that's the 5th November before Claire disappeared in the following February. He told the police in 1990 that he saw Claire there with a boy. He told the paper it made an impression on him because he had not thought she was that type of girl."

"Excuse me! What type of girl?" Priya is outraged on Claire's behalf; what's wrong with being in a café?

"The type that goes to coffee bars, I suppose! He couldn't be sure of the age of the boy she was with but he did see that he had a motor bike helmet."

"Aha!" says Priya, seeing the helmet as a solid clue at last.

"And what did the police make of Alex when they looked into it?" Priya sounds excited now.

"Apparently he was out of the frame" as Rita says this, Priya's excitement evaporates. "He said at the funeral that he had been to Bradgate Park a couple of times with Claire, in November and December he said. He hadn't arranged to meet her there on that day, in February."

"But there's only his word for it?" Priya is still keen on the Alex theory.

"Well, except that he was at the shoe shop that Saturday, the last day she was seen, and he went out to a folk concert with his mother in the evening. She met him from work so he was never alone."

"Could he have slipped over to Bradgate Park in his lunch hour? He did have a motor bike after all." Priya does not want to let go of her theory.

"That's what I thought, but then I found out that he didn't have his bike with him that day, because he was going out with his mother later. He could have met her another day, I suppose," Rita makes an equivocal gesture with her hand to indicate she thinks this less likely, "But that doesn't make much sense. At the funeral he seemed genuinely upset. Even after all this time, it's as if her disappearance was a source of genuine sadness to him."

"Glad to know his mother's still going strong. Is he married?" Priya inquires.

"Funnily enough, to a lady called Claire." Rita answers. She had elicited this from Alex before they parted company at the funeral.

"Weird!" is all Priya can manage, then "Are there more suspects?" Priya is prepared to entertain other ideas now.

"Well I guess we have to put this Mr Clarke in the frame – ha ha – he was the art teacher." Rita jokes, "and Mr Gregson, bless him, he did see her that last day. Then there's the bus conductors, any bus passengers, and anyone who happened to see her and decide to follow her. Or a random stranger who was in the Park."

"I guess you have to check out the father too. So many possibilities!" Priya teases.

"Your mum won't be pleased to hear you are still spending so much time on this instead of school work."

"Better solve it by the time I get back, we have exams soon. Have you tried RSVP?" Priya offers. "Sources and Voices, Beliefs and Practices."

"Oh" says Rita, glad to have another approach.

"Let's do it together" Priya offers, since this is more enticing than a discussion about chickpeas.

"Headings." says Rita, starting to make more notes "What do we know?"

"How do we know it?" asks Priya.

"Beliefs at the time?"

"Society at the time?"

"Hmmn, seems a bit excessive for just 40 years ago, but look at the changes to our families in that time!" Rita exclaims.

"So - family life. Good place to start." Priya is warming to her theme.

"What did Claire's father do?"

"Her brothers said he worked in a knitting factory in Wigston; he basically kept an eye on the people doing the work. He used to bike over there. He went out early with the boys to take them swimming on the Saturday she disappeared. He was with them all day. That was verified by the police in 1990." Rita explains.

"And her mother?"

"According to Thomas and Gerald, Claire's brothers, she gave up her nurse's training to get married and had odd jobs to fit in with the children. She wasn't as resourceful as your mother." (Mrs. Shah, Priya's mother, runs an internet clothes business from home.)

"She did deliveries for a flower shop, for example, and tried to sell things on the telephone – they had to be quiet while she was doing that, the phone was in the hall! And she worked on the traffic survey."

"What's one of those?"

"I had to ask Mr Thatcher. He said it's where they observe traffic usage on a particular stretch of road; so they know whether to build another one, like that toll road on the M6."

"What, someone has to sit by the road and count?" Priya is incredulous.

"That's probably how they did it then." Rita explains patiently. "Nowadays they mostly use technology of course - sensors on the road, computers and all that sort of thing. But in the seventies there wasn't the IT."

But it was hardly well paid work, Rita thinks.

"What about Claire? What school did she go to? What did she want to do?"

Rita explains she went to a school in town which had a different name then. It was girls only and at that time a grammar school; a few years later it started the process of becoming a mixed comprehensive college so that by the time the twins were 11 they were able to go there too. They said Claire liked drawing. "Maybe she had artistic ambitions?" Rita speculates.

"Was Claire happy at home? Could she have wanted to leave?" Priya is exploring possibilities.

"I gathered from Claire's brothers that it wasn't an idyllic childhood. Their mother was very strict. There were lots of rows. Sometimes she hit the twins with a wooden spoon they told me! There were days when her parents hardly spoke according to them, or spoke only to argue." Rita explains.

"Why not leave each other if they were so unhappy? Would they have found divorce difficult? They weren't Catholics for example?" Priya ponders the sensitive subject of relationship breakdown again. Being in Mumbai has reinforced for her the traditional roots to which her parents belong. Is that where she belongs? Does she have any choice? These ideas are at the back of her mind.

"Divorce just wasn't so common then. And what would Claire's mother have lived on? Her work can't have been well paid. I expect they must both have felt trapped." Rita is thinking aloud. "In fact I'm sure they must have felt that; did I tell you she was pregnant when they married?"

"Oh dear." says Priya, "Not a good start." Then, "Is there any evidence to support Claire's statement that she meant to leave."

"According to the postcard she was running away with this person called John." Rita reminds her friend.

"If she was going to do that, wouldn't she have had more stuff with her? I wouldn't run away without my iPad and straighteners!"

"Fair point." Rita concedes. "Nothing else was found apart from the few bits I told you about."

"Did the brothers know if anything was missing from her room?" Priya asks. Looking round the sparse guest room in her uncle's house, the empty table and wardrobe, Priya thinks of her own, cluttered, bedroom back in Loughborough and all the clothes and shoes she values, her books and music.

"There did not seem to be from what the brothers could remember, although they were only six at the time." Rita explains "They did say that it turned out her passport was missing – they said there was a terrible fuss when her parents found that out- a few days after the postcard came –but the passport wasn't with her body."

"Would it have disintegrated, in the ground?" Priya who has forensic ambitions is trying to piece together the picture.

"Hard to say, but you'd think the photo at least might have survived?"

"So the only source for the information is Claire herself?" Priya points out. "She went to Bradgate Park for unknown reasons, took her passport, wrote the post card and somehow posted it even though she was dead?"

"That's about the size of it." admits Rita with a sigh.

Chapter

14

"I pray you dispatch me quickly."
                    Lady Jane Grey to her executioner.

5ᵗʰ July 1971

They got to the beach at 10.30am. This was a family tradition. As was the trek across the sand, with Claire's father occasionally putting his hand to his eyes to scan the vista, hoping he struck a figure like Peter O'Toole in Lawrence of Arabia but succeeding, with his socks emerging from his sandals and hairy legs above them, to bring off a less glamorous effect. When he had pronounced on an optimal spot – not too near the sea, not too distant, not too near the kiosks, and reasonably far away from other people - they moved to the appointed place and set up camp, Claire and the boys laying out the rug, her father beginning to unroll and erect the windbreak, having taken readings with his finger as to the wind direction. Melanie then sat on the rug with her legs curled under her in a pose she had seen in a magazine.

When the construction work was done, the twins began digging - soon a large hole would appear and the others would have to take care not to fall into it – while Melanie poured everyone a cup of milky coffee from a flask. There were ginger biscuits too, which the boys enthusiastically bit into. The coffee and the biscuits were welcome, as was the shelter of the wind break. Although it was the first week of July - the start of the Leicester fortnight, when the textile factories, of which there were now dwindling numbers, had traditionally closed and the schools likewise – the temperature was only moderately warm and the wind blowing across the east coast was as ever keen. Mel and Phil divided the newspaper, the Daily Telegraph, between them and Claire lay on her side reading her book – Jane Austen's Sense and Sensibility.

They were staying in a Victorian terraced house in Cromer, about 15 minutes' walk from the beach. It was a small house – all that they could afford from the brochure Claire's mother had sent for. Claire was sleeping in the couch in the front room and the boys were on lilos in the back room, which doubled as the room where they ate, being off the scullery and bathroom. Melanie and Philip had the only bedroom, at the top of narrow stairs accessed through a wooden door with a metal latch, like a secret room or priest's hiding place. It made a change from home Claire thought. Good to be by the sea and have the chance to get a tan if the sun would come out for long enough!

Two men in their twenties walked by, quite near the encampment but circling round the boat shaped hole that Thomas and Gerald had made. They gave Claire's bare legs an approving look as they passed. Claire was engrossed in the way Mrs Dashwood was dealing with Marianne's emotional breakdown and failed to notice. What would her mother say if she, Claire, had a fit of the vapours?

"Claire?" Melanie's voice broke through the skin of her day dream "I think you should put a towel over your legs." Her mother tossed a rather worn white bath towel across the rug. "You don't want to get burnt." Melanie, unlike her daughter, had noted the unwanted attention.

After a lunch of potted meat sandwiches (made by Mel that morning) and chocolate biscuits, Phil got out his camera and positioned his family, like David Bailey on a photo shoot, "Don't lark about boys, you'll waste the film." He admonished the twins. Claire was in her swimming costume by now and the curve of her hips and contrast with her narrow waist, together with her full breasts, could be made out in her silhouette. Melanie, in a loose fitting Airtex t-shirt and nylon trousers, looked over at her daughter and frowned. The camera clicked. The boys had been giggling at some in joke they were sharing. Only Claire was staring full in to the camera.

* * *

After the photo they began to stride to the sea itself, which had receded a long way into the distance but was now according to Phil on the turn and coming in again. He was in the habit at the beginning of every holiday of studying the tide times; possibly it was the novelty which attracted him, coming as he did from the Midlands. 'Always swim when the tide's coming in' was one of his phrases; on the day trip he and Melanie had taken to Mablethorpe a swimmer had got into difficulties and drowned. This still made Phil shudder; you shouldn't take the sea for granted.

Carefully they picked their bare feet across the shingle and sharp shells. Claire feared the feel of a pebble digging into the ball of her foot which she could remember was very unpleasant, almost numbing, so she wanted to avoid having that experience again. The twins were running ahead, heedless. They moved so fast the pebbles would not get a chance to hurt them, and their feet were small. Phil was running after the twins, anxious that they should not plunge too quickly in to the waves but should adopt his zen-like approach of slow immersion which he found helped him adjust to the change of temperature. He knew Claire would follow. She was a sensible girl.

Claire was not very confident about walking to the sea in her costume. She would have preferred to keep the towel round her, but then there was nowhere to put it when she got to the sea. She knew where the anxiety came from. When she was 8 and they went on holiday, before the twins were born, she'd left the beach to buy sweets at the kiosk near the entrance. While she was waiting to pay, a man – a stranger - had slapped her on the bottom. Claire was surprised. What did he do that for? The man said something she didn't quite catch "Sight for sore eyes" something like that and another man winked lasciviously. Claire didn't understand what any of it meant, but it made her feel uncomfortable and self-conscious. She had never mentioned the incident to anyone.

Melanie, alone on the rug like abandoned Ariadne, watched the figures of her family getting smaller and mingling with those of other would-be bathers as well as those emerging from the sea, bedraggled but exultant, glowing on the inside and shivering on the outside. Melanie saw two teenage boys make their way across the shingle to Claire. Like three statues they stood a while, forming a circle, the boys each offered Claire a hand and helped her towards the safety of the soft wet sand. Melanie's frown deepened.

"You're not from here?" the boy called Mark asked Claire. "No, just on holiday. That's my Dad and brothers." she added in case they thought she was on her own.

"Staying anywhere nice?" this was the fair haired boy Kevin.

"Just a house. We're self-catering."

"How long are you here for, Claire?" Mark again as they cleared all the shingle.

The boys let go of her hands but the three continued to walk slowly as they talked. Her Dad was waist high in the water now, his ritual immersion well under way, and the twins were swimming into the waves as they rolled towards them, laughing and daring each other to go in further. They and Claire, at her father's insistence, were strong swimmers; he took them for lessons at the local swimming baths on Saturday mornings.

The trio reached the edge and Claire obligingly squealed at the feel of the cold sea on her warm toes. The three ran in and out a few times until the boys extended their hands again and led Claire into the crashing waves.

* * *

"Who were they?!" Melanie wanted to know as Claire, Thomas, Gerald and Philip sat shivering in towels on the now damp rug, Phil was rubbing at his thinning hair with a corner of his towel. Melanie was simultaneously helping the twins to dry themselves while staring at Claire accusingly.

"You shouldn't be talking to strange boys." she added before Claire could reply.

"They're called Kevin and Mark and they live here. Just two streets from where we're staying." her daughter supplied.

"You didn't tell them where we're staying?" Melanie was anxious.

"Not the number, no, just the road." Claire tried to be factual and avoid sounding annoyed,

"I should think so! We don't know anything about them." Melanie used self-righteous tones.

"They go to school here. They're in the sixth form. Kevin wants to do French at University and Mark's hoping to do Geography." Claire replied, not intending to contradict her mother. She had noted the reproving tone in Melanie's voice and decided that giving away more information would be like adding petrol to the flames. She did not mention, therefore, that Kevin and Mark said they would look out for her the next day. Claire liked the idea of spending some time with people of her own age, if she could manage to get away, although she was mentally comparing the boys' lack of maturity with Alex, who she had seen at the shoe shop where she worked on Saturdays. Alex seemed a lot older, although it was only by a couple of years, and she had been flattered when he had spoken to her, amazed he had noticed her at all. Claire put her towel over her face while she considered what of her not extensive holiday wardrobe she would wear to the beach tomorrow. Should she wear makeup? Mum would go mad if she saw her but the Jackie comics lent to her by Christine across the road said boys like girls to wear lipstick. Perhaps she'd sneak some on when Mum wasn't looking?

The boys had wriggled out of their trunks, which lay like black slugs on the rug.

"Phil, put the trunks on the wind break to dry." Melanie barked as she stood holding a towel round her daughter so she could affect the transformation from mermaid to human. Philip, who had changed already, started to tease Claire. "Come on, get your sexy shorts on."

"Phil" Melanie hissed. "There's no need to draw attention to her. Hurry up, Claire." she added impatiently.

Claire had found the cloying costume hard to prise off her salt-encrusted skin and was now struggling with equal difficulty to get cotton underwear over her not quite dry surface area. Her knickers kept rolling up when she tried to get her legs into them and she could not get her bra to do up. At last she had her t-shirt on and Melanie let go of the towel. The twins gave a wolf whistle and giggled at their sister in her t-shirt and knickers. "Oh shut up!" Claire said well humouredly as she pulled on her shorts. They left the beach at 4.30 so Mel could prepare the evening meal – which tonight would be macaroni cheese and tinned peaches. As they walked back to the house Phil was trying to remember how many photos were left on his film, and the twins were arguing over who should go in goal first when they got back. Melanie was thinking she needed to get some new clothes for Claire at the next jumble sale, those shorts were getting too tight. Claire was wondering if she would see Mark and Kevin the next day.

Chapter

15

"Lord, into thy hands I commend my spirit!"
Last words of Lady Jane Grey.

15ᵗʰ January 2013

The day is cold. Snow has settled on the pavements and roads and refuses to thaw. Cars slide like metal toys on a tin tray and drivers lose their grip trying to turn corners. A woman is crushed as a lorry skids on the main road and pins her to the wall. Most schools, including Rita's, are closed. Rita, snug in her centrally heated bedroom is talking to Priya on the phone. She has her friend on loud speaker so she can look at her iPad at the same time.

"So what mark did you get for your last essay?" Priya asks, knowing it had a Russian theme.

"I'm getting better." Rita replies. "I managed to find several conflicting sources about what happened to Tsar Nicholas and his family. The main thing was to identify the relevant facts – so hard when there are other issues people want to build theories around."

"The story about Anastasia surviving the massacre being one?" her friend asks, recalling in her mind the cartoon version.

"Yes, Because not all the bodies were found, the conspiracy theories started."

"Didn't Prince Philip give some DNA?" Priya recalls hearing about this.

"He did. Just like Claire's brothers." Rita adds, looking at the notes she has made on what happened to Claire.

"People believe what they want to believe." says Priya who

is combing one of her long brown bunches of hair again.

"Like Claire's family thinking she was in Scotland all that time." replies Rita.

"How many in the family were killed?" Priya asks.

"7 in all. The Tsar and Tsarina, of course, and then there were 5 children. The Tsarevitch was 13 by then-"

"The haemophiliac one? How sad that he was killed in the end." says Priya sympathetically.

"His sisters, Olga and Tatiana were in their twenties. Marie and Anastasia were teenagers. Young. Caught up in the politics. Like Lady Jane Grey."

Rita pauses, thinking about Claire again.

"The people who did it probably panicked afterwards – realised the enormity of what they'd done, they may even have been superstitious. They may have *said* they no longer saw the family as divinely protected, but who knew what the consequences of killing them might be- what if their scepticism was misplaced?"

"Which is why they botched disposal of the bodies?" inquires Priya, addressing her comb to the other bunch of hair.

"That's the theory, now. They tried unsuitable spaces as graves and ended up not putting them all together."

"How sad" Prya says again. "Why did it take the authorities so long to get to the truth? It was relatively recently wasn't it?"

"Yes, as the communist regime collapsed. The last body – possibly Anastasia or one of her sisters- was found in 2007 and a DNA test was done in 2009. I guess before then the authorities didn't want to probe too much. It was an event they maybe weren't too proud of. I expect the powers that be decided 'no further action.'"

"Hmmn," says Priya, seeing similarities with another historical event, "Like Henry VII never investigated the death of the princes in the tower. He probably knew where the bodies were buried, ha ha."

"No more extra essays anyway." Priya adds after a pause, conscious that her friend is not responding.

"Uhuh" Rita is not paying attention.

"Think school will be open tomorrow? I suppose it depends on the weather and if they clear the roads. It's because the teachers can't get in while the roads are bad. I 'spect Nayan's pleased, more time for his Nintendo DS."

Silence from Rita.

"So any more thoughts about Claire?" Priya has guessed where her friend's mind is.

"Mmmn?" Rita is distracted, looking at her notes.

Suddenly she sits up on her bed. "Oh yes." she says in a dream-like voice, her brain working as her voice speaks, "I think I see now, How tragic."

* * *

18th February 2013

It is half term. The snow is long gone and the air is mild but damp, with showers forecast for later. Rita, Priya and Nayan have taken the bus from Priya's house and are now walking purposefully across the shiny green and brown ground of Bradgate Country Park towards the ruins of the house. Soon they can see the red brick remains rising and falling in a jagged outline against the horizon. Spaces remind them that there were once windows and doors, the brickwork delineates fireplaces and chimneys. The only part recognisable as a building is the chapel. The rest is roofless and shapeless, like an abstract painting, or an installation at the Tate. In the distance, deer the colour of the bricks stand and stare at the three figures climbing over the remains of the great house.

In the cloud-like air, their breath turns to vapour as the

three walk and talk. Ghosts are whispering everywhere. Rita can picture Claire and Alex sitting on a wall talking together in low tones, Lady Jane Grey and her sisters are studiously at their lessons, her severe mother Frances and power-hungry father John are in another corner, plotting together how to put Jane on the throne, and who to marry the girls to. They would have looked out of these gaping window spaces onto the park and seen a glittering future; how quickly it all descended into disaster and disappointment. How sad that young lives were extinguished just as they were starting.

"I don't know why we had to come out here." Nayan spoils the mood Rita was creating in her head. "We can't come here on our own." Priya explains again "My mother would not like it. So you are our alibi."

"Alibi?" Nayan is not sure this is the right word.

"Bodyguard, then." He prefers this.

"We'll buy you chips on the way back." Rita knows the way to her brother's heart.

* * *

Before deciding to contact Claire's brothers again, Rita visited the temple with her mother and said various prayers which she had read were helpful in relation to a violent death. She thought it would not matter that the death was so long ago. Rita is fond of the temple which she and her mother approached, their heads covered, garlands in their hands ("Perhaps you can get this Claire business out of your system now", said Padma afterwards, "you don't want it to distract you from your studies"). Entering the temple reminded Rita of the excitement and joy when it had been opened the year before last. There had been a colourful procession with dancers whirling, drums beating, instruments playing. The gods were taken to their new home, (Brahma the creator, Vishnu the preserver, Shiva the destroyer, among others) a magical mix of traditional and modern designs and techniques, the outside of the temple rivalled in beauty the well-known temple in Neasden and the interior was so richly and delicately decorated that it vied with any in Rajasthan. Like a Hindu version of Hagia Sophia in Istanbul her religious studies teacher had said when they went on a school trip there.

The temple visit had helped Rita to feel calm as the anticipated phone call approached. She has arranged for the twins to call her. Settling on a low wall among the ruins of the house, Rita and Priya arrange a rug beneath them while Nayan plays with his football. The denim-clad legs of the girls dangle against the old brick work. Priya takes out her comb and Rita takes a deep breath as her phone rings as arranged. Thomas and Gerald are on holiday in Singapore, so eight hours away.

"Hi Rita" they both say over the loud speaker. "How's the weather with you guys? We heard it was pretty bad."

Their antipodean tones echo strangely in this ancient place; incongruous in a location when Rita can envisage women in long ornately brocaded dresses and men in doublet and hose.

"We had snow." She tells them "You know what it's like. A few inches and everything comes to a halt. But it's melted now."

"That's good." They say "Can't remember what snow is like. It's been a while. So hot here."

"I'm not sure I want to know that!" Rita laughs. Then she clears her throat, changing the mood.

"I'm at Bradgate Country Park now, with my friend Priya, in the ruins of the house built by Lady Jane Grey's father. I wanted to ask you something."

"OK".

"Apart from family outings, did your mother ever take you to Bradgate Park?"

"No." Tom answers first as usual.

"Wait," Gerry this time

"She did you know. Don't you remember?" Gerry continues. "One afternoon. Not long after bonfire night, she picked us up from school and said we were going on an adventure for a change. She drove to Bradgate and parked in a lay-by opposite the car park. Mother got out of the car and left us in it, don't you remember?"

"Vaguely." Thomas again. "Was it November? I remember being fed up that she wouldn't let us out".

"And when she got back in the car she was in a very bad mood."

"You couldn't argue with her in one of her moods."

"I don't want to upset you," says Rita, taking a deep breath, "but think who had power over the main aspects of the story of Claire's disappearance."

"Well, Claire you mean?" Thomas asks.

"Depends what you think the main aspects are I guess." Gerry this time.

"I narrowed it down to this" says Rita, "what I call the 4 Ps."

"OK." Thomas is curious. "What are those?"

Rita explains,

"1. The post card - it came after Claire disappeared.

2. The passport - it disappeared when or after Claire was last seen.

3. The police. They started to investigate, then were called off. No one tried to find her again until you did in 1990.

4. The Park. You used to go regularly on family outings, then you stopped after Claire was last seen. And you were brought here in the November before she vanished."

"Mmmnhh" The brothers are trying to see what Rita is driving at.

"Who controlled these things?" Like a round of 'Only Connect' Thomas and Gerald are talking aloud to try to see what the 4 P's might have in common'.

"Start with the Park." Gerald suggests this time, "Our parents decided where we went. Well mother did really. Dad just went along with what she wanted, anything for a quiet life."

"The police were called off when the post card arrived so those two are linked. I guess it was mother who put her foot down about not looking for Claire. That's why we only did it when she was too ill to object." Thomas summarises.

"The postcard and the passport?" Gerald speaks "Could mother have influenced those?"

"One interesting fact about the passport and the postcard is that both these items disappeared completely." Rita hints.

Slowly, the penny is dropping, she can hear.

"I suppose we only had mother's word that the passport was gone. So she could have taken it. Is that what you mean?" Gerald again, "And she could have sent the postcard?"

"It fits." Is all Rita says. Let the truth rise to the surface she thinks.

"Yes", says Thomas slowly with a sigh "I guess it all fits."

There is a silence from thousands of miles away for a few instants.

* * *

Later, on the bus back to her house, Priya eventually speaks. Rita knows by her friend's silence that her brain has been in overdrive since the phone call.

"Hang on." Priya says, touching Rita on the arm, "Are you saying her own mother did Claire harm? Killed her in the Park and left her there?"

"Well" Rita says slowly "I don't want to say she definitely did, but…" turning to face Priya, Rita continues, "She knew Claire met her boyfriend Alex there – she may have seen her by accident when she was doing the traffic survey. I think that's what she witnessed when she took the brothers to the Park in November; and on the day Claire disappeared her mother either knew Claire was going there again, or followed her, or…" Rita continues.

"Or lured her there with a forged note?" Nayan this time. He is sitting behind the girls and leans forward between them to join in the discussion.

"But she wouldn't have meant to kill her!" Nayan adds, incredulously.

"She probably didn't" Rita agrees "But imagine if she confronted Claire there, if there was an argument, if she just pushed Claire or struck her. The brothers said their mother could strike out. And, according to Mr Payne - your mum's osteopath - she is unlikely to have fallen or fainted in that way and banged her head. Say she was pushed or hit and went backwards, hit her head, stopped breathing."

"Their mother had been training to be a nurse, she would know it was bad." Priya again.

"Exactly. Then imagine she realised the enormity of it. Panicked and fled. People do panic after the event. They can behave quite irrationally."

"She couldn't have sent the postcard? Although I can see that she could have forged the writing I suppose." Priya is picturing the events.

"after her night school classes in calligraphy." Rita adds, then as Priya shakes her head and Nayan says. "How did she post it?"

Rita addresses her friend and brother, gloved hands animatedly illustrating her argument.

"What if she used one of the blank chain letter ones?" she pauses while the others consider this. "She could have copied Claire's writing easily. All she would need to do is smudge or alter the date on the post mark. No one would be looking at it that closely, I don't suppose. It wasn't like *Silent Witness* then."

"So all that time she knew Claire was never coming back?" there is a wistful tone in Priya's voice

"I think it's possible" says Rita quietly. "It's pretty unthinkable but it works as a theory. It explains why she was so adamant that they shouldn't look for her. Why she was not waiting for her to call. Only the trees at the place she fell knew the secret, and they kept it for 40 years".

* * *

A week later, the brothers send flowers and a card to Rita. It reads "Thanks for all your help. We think your theory may be the right one. We are not pressing the police to solve what happened. We've asked for no further action. Probably we will never know for sure".

Rita writes back -

"Sorry to come to such a conclusion. Be brave." She wrote on a card she got from a shop near the temple. On the front was printed:

*"The goal in life is self-realisation.
The truth will set you free."*

*Rita Patel returns in
Body in the lake*

ISBN: 978-1-910779-72-9

ISBN: 978-1-910779-73-6

ISBN: 978-1-910779-74-3

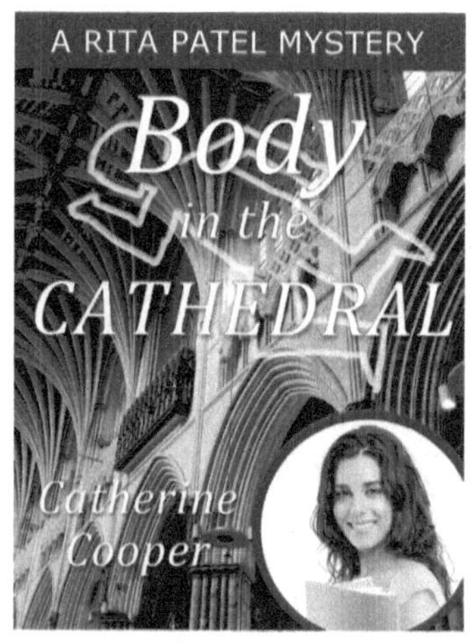

ISBN: 978-1-910779-75-0